Al's Blind Date

OTHER BOOKS BY CONSTANCE C. GREENE

A Girl Called Al
The Unmaking of Rabbit
Isabelle the Itch
Isabelle Shows Her Stuff
Isabelle and Little Orphan Frannie
I Know You, Al
Beat the Turtle Drum
I and Sproggy
Your Old Pal, Al
Dotty's Suitcase
Double-Dare O'Toole
Al(exandra) the Great
Just Plain Al
Star Shine

Al's Blind Date

Constance C. Greene

Viking

VIKING
Published by the Penguin Group
Viking Penguin, a division of Penguin Books USA Inc.,
40 West 23rd Street, New York, New York 10010, U.S.A.
Penguin Books Ltd, 27 Wrights Lane, London W8 5TZ, England
Penguin Books Australia Ltd, Ringwood, Victoria, Australia
Penguin Books Canada Ltd, 2801 John Street, Markham, Ontario, Canada L3R 1B4
Penguin Books (N.Z.) Ltd, 182–190 Wairau Road, Auckland 10, New Zealand

Penguin Books Ltd, Registered Offices: Harmondsworth, Middlesex, England

First published in 1989 by Viking Penguin, a division of Penguin Books USA Inc.
10 9 8 7 6 5 4 3 2 1
Copyright © Constance C. Greene, 1989
All rights reserved

Library of Congress Catalog Card Number: 89-14639
(CIP information available upon request)
ISBN 0-670-82815-7

Printed in United States of America
Set in Aster.

*To all children
who love to read*

Al's Blind Date

One

"Blind Date! I would never never go on a blind date!"
Thelma cried, fluffing up her back hair so her bangle
bracelets jangled noisily.

"Blind dates are tacky. My mother says they were
tacky in her day and they still are. No really popular
girl"—and Thelma smiled complacently down at her
chest . . . "would be caught dead on a blind date."

It was Sunday. We were having lunch at Polly's.
Sunday is usually togetherness day for Al and her
mother, but today Al was off the hook due to the fact
her mother was whooping it up at some fancy do at
the Plaza.

Some days we discuss world affairs, some days politics. Today we were into blind dates.

"I don't believe I know any really popular girls, Thel," Al said, smiling. "And never say never, kid. It's bad luck."

"What's that you're cooking, Polly?" I asked.

"Hollandaise," Polly said. "For the eggs benedict. You have to stir it constantly or it'll lump up on you."

"Mr. Richards!" Al and I said in unison, on account of that's what he told us when he was teaching us to make white sauce.

"Eggs Benny," Thelma said. "Yum. What are you two, clones or something?" She was all bent out of shape, I think, probably because of what Al said about not knowing any really popular girls. Thelma's had six dates. Well, one doesn't count because it was with her cousin. She didn't tell us that; Polly did. Al doubts the other five bozos even exist but so far, nobody's been able to prove anything.

"Next thing you know," Thelma said, "you two will be wearing matching dresses or something nauseating like that." Thelma ruffled her back hair again and her bracelets got noisy. Thelma thinks her arms are sexy, Al says. But then, she also thinks her teeth and her elbows and other parts too numerous to mention are also sexy.

"Oh, we already have matching dresses," Al said. "We're very cute together. When we wear them, people think we're twins."

"What are they, dotted swiss with matching bloom-ers and puffed sleeves?" Thelma drawled.

"Actually," Al drawled back, "they're leather."

"Yeah," I spoke up. "Mine's red and hers is black."

"I don't believe it," Thelma snapped. "You two in leather dresses. I could die laughing."

"Try," Al said.

"Soup's on!" Polly shouted. *"Mange, mange!"* and we all filed to the stove carrying our plates.

"Eggs Benny are my very favorite, Polly," Thelma said. "Yum."

"Yum yum," Al said, stony faced.

We sat down and dug in.

"What would we do without you, Pol?" I said.

"Starve, probably," Polly said.

"I knew a boy named Benny in California," Al said. "He was an egghead too. He could already read in first grade. Benny was very smart, but on the first day of school he wet his pants and everybody laughed and he went home and didn't show up for a week. Our teacher told us we should be very careful about laugh-ing at someone because as sure as you're born, she said, we'd all do something embarrassing someday and then people would laugh at us and we'd know how Benny felt. She said we should be kind because there's too little kindness in this world. And she said everyone needs kindness. I never forgot that."

Polly nodded. "Little kids are very cruel sometimes. But so are big kids. I think you have to learn to be kind. I don't think you're born kind, I mean. I think you have to be taught kindness."

"Lots of adults are unkind, too," Al said. "It's not just kids. I don't think you learn it, I think it's in your genes. You're either born kind or you're not."

"Well, my mother says good manners and kindness sort of go hand in hand," I said. "That's why she's such a bug on good manners."

"This is turning into a very philosophical conversation," Thelma said in her bored way.

It *was* kind of philosophical, I thought, pleasantly surprised.

We all had seconds of the eggs Benny to clear our heads.

"Speaking of blind dates," Polly said, "Evelyn might get married to a guy she met on a blind date. She fell madly in love with him because he's got two little kids and if she marries him, that means she'll be a stepmother and she says she's always wanted to be a stepmother."

Evelyn is Polly's off-the-wall older sister.

"Who's she marrying?" Al said.

"He's this really nice guy, kind of old, about thirty-five or so," Polly said. "His wife left him to find herself."

"Suppose she finds herself and comes back? What then?" Al said. "Couldn't that get kind of hairy?"

"Who knows?" Polly said. "My father says Evelyn

changes her mind and her plans so often it doesn't pay to worry."

"Why does she want to be a stepmother?" Thelma asked.

"Well, she loves little kids and she figures if she's a stepmother, that means she doesn't have to have kids of her own, which means she won't get stretch marks," Polly told us.

"Stretch marks?" I said.

"They're what you get when you're pregnant," Polly explained. "The baby grows bigger and bigger, so your stomach stretches and it leaves marks on your stomach that don't go away. And Evelyn figures if she had stretch marks she could never wear a bikini again."

This was followed by a small silence while we all contemplated Evelyn in a one-piece suit complete with skirt.

"I'll have to think about that for a while, Polly," Al said. "Toss it around and see how it comes out. But listen to my blind-date story, which I think is very romantic. I read it last week. There's this dude called the earl of Wistwick, see. He meets some lovely on a blind date and marries her two weeks later, thereby renouncing his claim to the throne. He was sixteenth in line to the throne, you see, and she swept him off his feet and he's no longer sixteenth in line; he's nowhere. How about that for a blind date, huh?"

"Who's the earl of Wistwick, anyhow?" Thelma

asked, voicing the thoughts of us all. "And why'd he have to renounce his claims to the throne just because he got married?"

"I thought you'd never ask," Al said with a big grin. "He had to renounce his claim to the throne because royalty doesn't recognize divorce and the earl's bride is the divorced mother of two, that's why. She just swept him off his little feet. The earl is thirty-nine, you see, and his bride is twenty-five, so it was high time the earl got hitched."

There wasn't a whole lot to be said to that, so we finished our eggs Benny and waited for dessert.

Polly put a blue bowl with apples and pears in it in the center of the table.

"Fruit," Polly said.

"Fruit," said Al, who had hoped for lemon meringue pie. "*Parfait*. Fruit is very slimming, I hear."

"Yeah," Thelma said. "Take a few apples, Al."

"Who were the fifteen guys ahead of the earl?" I asked, seeing the storm clouds gather on Al's face. "That's a lot of guys lined up for the throne, if you ask me. I'd sure hate to be hanging by my thumbs until those other guys were eliminated. What's the big deal about renouncing his claim to the throne, anyway?"

"Listen, the earl was really into royalty," Al said. "He dreamed of the day when he'd hoist his scepter and don his ermine mantle and climb up there, master of all he surveyed. He also liked the perks, the trips on the royal yacht, stuff like that. Those were great eggs Benny, Polly."

Thelma turned to me and said, "Does she know this earl person? I mean, is he a personal friend or something?"

"Not that I know of," I said.

"I think that's a fabulous story, Al," said Polly. "Very romantic. To give everything up for love. Terrific."

Al beamed. "You've got it, Pol. Me too. I love it. And to think that they got it all together on a blind date. *Fantastic.* The crowning touch." She looked surprised, then said, "The crowning touch. Get it? *Parfait.*"

We all stared at Al.

"She's a très weird person," Thelma said.

"Well, I don't know about you guys," Al said, "but I can hardly wait for my first blind date. I can see him now, a superstar on a Yamaha, all in black leather, jacket and puttees and helmet, and me in my black leather dress. We'll ride into the sunset with his chains clanking like an armful of bracelets."

"That wasn't kind," I told Al on our way home. "You didn't have to say that about the bracelets."

"O.K., and she didn't have to say that about me taking some apples for slimming, either," Al said.

"Thelma's a bird," I said. "Ignore her."

"Yeah, a vulture," Al said. "I never should've had seconds. As a matter of fact, I never should've had firsts. I'm bulging."

9

When we got off at our floor, I asked Al if she wanted to come in and listen to my new tapes.

"No offense," she said, "but I've got to go weigh myself. If the earl of Wistwick landed me as his blind date, he'd still be single and sixteenth in line to the throne." She lifted a hand in salute.

"Have a weird day, comrade," she said.

I had a sudden, perfect thought.

"Hey," I said, "the earl's entitled, isn't he? I mean, if he wants to marry a divorced mother of two, he's entitled. Right?"

Al did a couple of bumps and grinds and grinned at me.

"You have unexpected depths, o skinny one," she said and went inside.

I never should've had seconds either, I decided.

TWO

When Al turned fourteen last month, she went into a tailspin. She decided Al was a babyish name. Plus it lacked class and pizzazz. So we thrashed around for a while, trying to come up with something jazzy: Zandra, Sandy, Alex.

Nothing fit.

Then she wrapped her head in a turban and decided to call herself Mother Zandi. When our homeroom teacher, Mr. Keogh, asked us to visit the old people's home his father was in, Al told fortunes in a deep, dark, swami-type voice. The seniors loved her. She wowed 'em. My father says you call that a boffo performance. Now, whenever she feels like it, Al turns into Mother Zandi, her alter ego, so to speak.

When I first knew her, Al was a little on the plump side. Then she stopped pigging out and dropped a lot of flesh. Al fights the battle of the bulge constantly. Right now, I think she's losing it. Again.

I'm not saying a word, but last week I think I saw Al's behind wiggle. In gym class. I thought I should tell her, then I rethought and kept my mouth shut. If there's one thing that drives Al bonkers, it's a behind that wiggles; her own or anyone else's.

In the early days of our friendship, Al wore Chubbies.

Chubbies, according to Al, are a fate worse than death.

Al's mother, since she works in Better Dresses and all, is extremely weight and fashion conscious. She thinks if you're more than a size ten you better shape up or ship out.

Next morning Al was waiting in the lobby with a long face.

"Check this," she said, pulling up her sweater to show me the safety pin holding her skirt closed.

"Nice, huh?" Al said, glum as could be. "I knew I never should've had seconds at Polly's. My mother will flip. It's brand new. She'll probaby send me to a fat farm for my Christmas present."

"Maybe the fat farm will be near where Brian lives," I said, trying to look on the bright side.

"You're a riot," she said.

"I wasn't trying to be," I said. "It just happened."

"It's creeping avoirdupois," Al grumbled. "There's no sense kidding myself. I could lie, say the skirt must've shrunk at the cleaners, except it hasn't been to the cleaners. I'm headed for the fat farm, that's for sure. Along with the rest of the cows."

Al has lots of ups and downs. I'm always cheering her up. Or trying to. Al's very demanding. I have to stand by her. She's my best friend. In the long run, she's worth it. It's just that in the short run I sometimes run out of steam.

With her stomping along, muttering to herself, and me bringing up the rear, you should pardon the expression, we set off for school.

I was right. Her behind *did* wiggle. Oh, boy. I hoped no one but me would notice. I prayed no one would say anything to her.

When Al gets in the pits, she zones out. Tunnel vision takes over. She started to cross against the light at Eighty-sixth Street and a taxi driver yelled at her. She blinked and tugged nervously at her skirt.

"I thought when I became fourteen I'd have it made," Al said. "But no, it's the same old rat race. The same old ugly face in the mirror, the same old head of hair full of split ends. Instead of a face lift, maybe I oughta get a head lift. You know, a whole new head. Something plastic surgeons have not yet come to grips with. Whaddaya think?"

"Well," I said, "if you keep walking in front of cabs, something's bound to happen. You might wind up in the emergency room. Where you would then meet a most adorable intern. I understand lots of interns are adorable and mostly unmarried on account of they're married to their jobs and don't have time for romance."

"Who does?" Al said. "Romance is on its way out. Romance is dead. Romance is kaput. People never send other people a dozen long-stemmed roses anymore. Or a box of chocolates. When was the last time somebody sent you a dozen long-stemmed roses or chocolates? When, I ask you."

She stopped walking and stared at me.

"Me?" I said. "*Moi?*" Well . . ." I pretended to think. "Let's see."

"You're such a turkey," Al sighed. "I bet you never even got a Valentine from a boy."

"Sure I have. From my father. He's a boy, isn't he?"

Al snorted. "I bet Brian's not sending me a Valentine. Probably he's ditched me for a girl who plays the tuba in the school band and has this cool uniform with brass buttons and wears little white boots with tassels on 'em."

"If she totes a tuba, she must be pretty strong," I said.

Al scowled at me and I could see I'd said the wrong thing.

"Don't sweat it," I told her. "Valentine's Day is ages away. I wouldn't worry if I was you."

"Your problem is," Al said in a cool voice, "you are

the kind of person who goes through life blithely without a worry in your pointed little head. You make me sick."

"Yeah, well, you make me sick too," I said. "You worry enough for both of us. You should be more like me; fat, dumb, and happy, then you'd . . ."

If I could've bitten off my tongue, I would've. What a thing to say to Al, of all people. Fat, dumb, and happy was just an old-fashioned expression I'd heard my mother use. It didn't mean anything personal. It didn't mean Al was any of those things. But I knew, from the way she hunched her shoulders and put her head down as she ran up the school steps, that I'd been tactless. One more time.

When I got to our homeroom, Al wasn't there. Our new homeroom teacher, Ms. Bolton, was at her desk, marking papers. I feel sorry for Ms. Bolton. So does Al. She doesn't seem to have made friends. The other teachers are polite but not particularly friendly. Once Al and I were on the bus and we saw Ms. Bolton walking with a man. She looked really happy, the only time I've seen her look that way.

Ms. Bolton wears big baggy sweaters, full skirts, and red tights. Almost every day she wears the same thing. I think she might change her luck if she changed the color of her tights. I would like to suggest this to her but feel it's none of my business. Al and I have decided that she must be one of those people who, through no fault of her own, doesn't relate to others.

Al says that, psychologically, Ms. Bolton is the sort others shun. She read about this sort of person in some medical journal and she's decided that's Ms. Bolton's problem. I think we should do something to try to help her. But I don't know exactly what.

"Hello, Ms. Bolton," I said. She raised her head and for a minute I don't think she registered. Her eyes looked blank. Then she came to, said hello back to me, and went on working. She's not much for small talk, I guess.

I went to my desk and began to clean it out. Even though we'd only been back at school a few weeks, it was already crammed with junk. I'm basically quite untidy. I mean, I can live with a mess. But because I wanted to keep busy, I made a big show of gathering up some gum wrappers and scratch sheets I'd doodled on and carrying them up to the wastebasket.

Ms. Bolton went on working. I might have been the Invisible Man, for all she noticed.

Then, as I made my way back to my desk, I heard her make a funny noise. "Sorry?" I said, turning to look at her. Her head was down on her desk. Then Al showed up. It was me and her and Ms. Bolton in the room.

"*Que passe?*" Al said.

"Maybe she's sick," I said.

Ms. Bolton's head stayed down. I think she was crying. Her shoulders moved, but she didn't make a sound.

Al went to her and touched her on the arm.

"Can we help?" she said. I wish I'd thought of doing or saying that.

Ms. Bolton lost it then. Completely. I mean, she bawled. Really loud.

"You think we should call somebody?" I asked Al.

Ms. Bolton must've heard. "No," she said, raising her head. "Please. I'll be all right. Just give me a minute."

Tears streamed down her face. Her hair was wild. So were her eyes.

"I'll get some water," Al whispered and she skinned out. I stayed put, not knowing what else to do.

Ms. Bolton took a few gulps of air and shook her hair out of her eyes.

"I'm all right, really," she said. She blew her nose and smiled weakly at me. "My life just isn't what . . . well, it's hard to explain. It just isn't what I'd hoped. I'll get it together soon."

Al came back, saving me from having to reply.

"Here." Al thrust a small paper cup at Ms. Bolton.

"Thanks." She drained the cup and smiled a watery smile. "I'm sorry, kids. Thanks. I don't want to lay my problems on you. Do me a favor. Don't say anything about this to anyone, O.K.?"

We heard someone coming. Hastily, Ms. Bolton ran a comb through her hair and her face assumed a somewhat more cheerful look.

Wouldn't you know. Martha Moseley bustled in, full of herself, as usual.

"Ms. Bolton," she said, "I know it's not due until next week, but I did my English assignment early. I got carried away. My poem is about going to a graveyard and studying the gravestones, what they say." Martha slid her eyes sideways, checking to see if we were properly impressed.

"When I read my poem to my mother," Martha continued, "she actually cried. She was totally overcome at the beauty of it. The images. My father said I should send my poem to one of the little magazines. The ones that don't pay much but that, artistically, a true poet should aim for. Do you think I should, Ms. Bolton?"

"How about your father?" Al said. "Was he totally overcome too?"

"What's your poem going to be about, Alexandra?" Martha said in a snippy voice. "Eating popcorn at the movies?"

"Actually . . ." Al spoke so slowly I knew she was stalling for time. "Actually, it's shaping up pretty well. It's going to be an epic poem. Sort of like the *Iliad*. It relates a hero's advantages and accomplishments." From the rush of words, I knew Al had been inspired. She was really getting into it.

"An epic's very long, you see, Martha. You can't just dash it off. It takes a lot of time. Mine's an epic poem and the hero is Napoleon."

I gasped. She was going for the gold on this one, I thought. Napoleon was no small potatoes.

"There's been talk of making it into a film," Al said. Even Ms. Bolton looked impressed.

"Starring Michael J. Fox as Napoleon. They're about the same size. So he'd be perfect for the role. Michael J. Fox, I mean. My agent's working on it now."

Martha opened her mouth to say something, thought better of it, and bustled over to her desk. I thought I saw smoke coming out of her ears, but I couldn't be sure.

"Well done," I told Al. "That gives you one point for one-upmanship."

Ms. Bolton laughed a bit shakily.

"Sounds good, Al," she said. "I'll be eager to see the final results."

"Actually," Al said, frowning fiercely at the blackboard, "it's still in the planning stage. I'm still thinking it out in my head. I haven't actually written any of it yet."

"Actually, Al, I didn't think you had," Ms. Bolton said.

Three

"I can't get over her crying like that," Al said. We were on our way home, friends again. We never stay mad at each other for long.

"Who does that remind you of?" Al pushed her nose against the butcher's window. From his window displays, I'd say he's a very artistic butcher. Last week he had a whole pig with an apple stuck in its mouth. That pig had the saddest little eyes I ever saw. The week before that, a bunch of lamb chops dressed in frilly pantaloons danced in a circle. But today just a side of beef hung out, naked and alone.

"Martha Moseley," I said. That cracked us both up.

"Maybe she's broke," Al said after we'd calmed

down. I knew she meant Ms. Bolton, not Martha Moseley. "Teachers don't make big bucks, you know."

"No, I think it's her boyfriend," I said. "She wants him to make a commitment and he won't."

"Yeah, he's most likely the divorced father of two, and his kids don't like Ms. Bolton." Al gave me a piercer. "I think she must be very gullible and falls for any charlatan who buys her a beer. I don't think she knows squat about life."

"Not like us women of the world, you mean," I said. "Well, whatever's bothering her, we should try to help. But how?"

"Ah, you ask the cosmic question to which I do not have the cosmic answer," Al said. Then she grabbed me and hissed, "Look! Up Ahead! Do you see what I see?"

"It's only a man in a skirt," I said, yawning. "Big deal. Maybe his mother always wanted a girl."

"It's a bagpiper, you turnip," Al told me.

A man wearing kilts and carrying bagpipes over his shoulder came toward us. His face was wide and red and he had a bristling mustache.

"I bet he's from Scotland," Al said. "I absolutely love bagpipes. They sound so sad and desolate and they make me feel as if Laurence Olivier is chasing me across the moors, hollering, 'Cathy! Cathy!' at me."

"Laurence who?" I said.

"Laurence Olivier. Wuthering Heights. Heathcliff."

"Oh, that Laurence Olivier," I said, remembering. "Who's Cathy?"

"Merle Oberon, turd."

"Oh," I said again, smiling at the memory. "Trouble with that scenario is, kiddo, you don't look much like old Merle."

"You really know how to hurt a guy," Al grumbled.

The man in kilts must've seen us staring at him. As he drew near, he smiled and gave us a little salute.

"Are you from Scotland?" Al asked him. She can be pretty bold when it behooves her, I thought.

"That I am, lassie," he said. "Do you know Scotland, then?"

"Not really," Al said, blushing a little. "But I've read tons of books about it. I would love to go there someday. Some of my ancestors are Scottish. I'd like to see the moors and the heather. And I think I'd like to try some haggis."

"Ah, yes, haggis," the man said. "Oh, you make me miss it right this moment. I'm from Glasgow myself. I'm here in your great city for a few days and already I'm homesick and longing for a taste of it."

"What's haggis?" I said.

"It's the Scottish national dish, lass," he said to me. "It's the sheep's intestines boiled in its stomach along with a bit of oatmeal."

"I thought you'd never ask," Al said to me, grinning. I felt my stomach heave. I rejected the whole idea of haggis. Such a thing couldn't be true.

"I absolutely love the bagpipes," Al said, breathless.

In answer, the man blew us a few notes on his pipes. People stopped to listen. It was indeed a sad and lonely sound.

"Now that's a bonnie sound, isn't it?" the man said. "You'll not find a bonnier one if you travel the world over. You must come to Glasgow someday."

"Oh, I plan to," Al said. "When I save up enough money. I hear it's very beautiful and the people are really hospitable."

Any minute now, I thought, they'll start exchanging telephone numbers.

"That it is," the man agreed, and he saluted us again and walked away jauntily, skirts swinging as he shouldered his pipes.

"He has nice legs," I said, admiring him from afar. "Maybe we should've asked him if he was married. Maybe he's lonely. We could've fixed him up a blind date for Ms. Bolton."

"You're out of your gourd," Al said. "You can't ask a total stranger if he's married or if he'd like a blind date with your teacher. Suppose he's a serial killer or something. Just because he plays the bagpipes and has nice legs doesn't mean his heart is pure."

I had to admit she had a point.

"Maybe we should've warned him about Rockefeller Center," I said. "In those kilts he might be in tough shape." Rockefeller Center Plaza is a regular wind tunnel. Lots of folks have lost their wigs and umbrellas, and it can be dangerous once that wind gets under your skirt.

"It's got so I can't let you out of the house alone," Al said, glaring at me. "You're becoming very bold, know that?"

"Look who's talking," I said. "You're the one who picked him up, not me. I wonder if his underpants are plaid too, to match his kilt. I'd sure like to find out."

Al shook her head and *tch-tch*ed at me. "You have to admit he was pretty cute," she said. "A true Scottish gentleman. I dig that lassie routine, but I'm not sure he's Ms. Bolton's type. I bet she'd go more for the pretty type, like the guys in the Ralph Lauren ads."

"That type is very, very boring," I said. "They never smile and you know why? Because they're worried their tie is crooked or their socks don't match. Or their hair isn't on straight. They're not interested in you, their interested in them."

"How about if we suggest to Ms. Bolton she put one of those ads in the personals column in the paper?" Al suggested. "You know, 'caring nonsmoker, into sunsets and red setters.'"

"Talk about blind dates! That's about as blind as you can get, I figure," I said.

"They usually say 'photo a must,' " Al went on. "That's so you know what you're getting into. But suppose you're ugly as sin, your nose is all over your face, and you're snaggletoothed. What then?"

"You send in a photo of your beautiful sister," I said. "And the guy falls into instant love with her and writes back saying 'How about Saturday night?' What then?"

"Problems, problems," Al said airily. "Let's cross here. I want to check out the puppies in the pet shop. If my mother would let me, I'd take the brown-and-white one with the curly tail."

But the pet shop was gone, along with the puppies. In its window a big sign said

FREE OFFER! SEE INSIDE! TIGHTEN YOUR BOD!
FURM, TONE, IMPROVE YOUR SHAPE!
JOIN AL'S HEALTH CLUB.
FREE OFFER! SEE INSIDE!

A man with a big belly stood in the doorway, yelling at the moving men.

"Watch it! Break that and it'll cost ya!" he hollered.

"That must be Al," Al said. "Not only is he an entrepreneur in the fitness game, he's also a heck of a speller. Check 'firm.' Should we tell him?"

"I like it that way," I said. "Check the abs and the gluts," I whispered. "How about the pecs?" Al whispered back. That cracked us up.

The man with the big belly wandered over to us. "Let us in on the joke, girls."

"Begging your pardon, sir," Al said.

The fat man's lips moved in a twitchy way. Was he smiling?

Al has this theory that if you address people as 'sir' they immediately like you because they think you respect them.

"Begging your pardon, sir," she said again. She'd been reading *The Return of the Native;* that's the way they talked in Thomas Hardy's day.

Sure enough, I noticed that every time she called him sir he looked a little less threatening. His was a face that only a mother could love. That was one of my mother's expressions, some of which are quite good. Al gave them another shot of "Begging your pardon, sir," which I figured was overdoing it. By the time she'd finished with him, he wore a big smile; probably a first for him.

"What's on your mind, girlie?" he asked Al.

"What happened to the pet shop?" Al said. "It was here only last week. We came to see the puppies, sir."

That was it for the sirs. The guy was soft as a grape by now.

"Gonzo," he said gruffly. "The guy can't handle the rent raise. He's gotta pack up his pooches and split. It's no skin off my nose. I'm in for a bundle, all this high-class machinery. Borrowed from my mother-in-law. She gives me a break, charges ten percent interest instead of her usual twenty. What a sweetheart.

"Hey!" he hollered as the moving men carried a big machine across the sidewalk. "That's a cross-country ski simulator," he told us proudly. "All that and more is what you're gonna find inside. You want a free tryout, you got it. You from around here?"

We nodded, although it wasn't really our neighborhood.

"Inside we got our tanning machine, you wanna glow all year long," he said. "We also got available shiatsu and Swedish massage. Not to mention an Olympic weight room complete with a roto curl bar and a squat rack."

"Hey, neat," Al said.

"What's a squat rack?" I asked but got no answer.

"Sounds good, sir." Al dealt the coup de grace with her final sir. He was hers.

"Come by tomorra, why dontcha? Just ask for me and you'll try our equipment, then spread the word that Al's is the best of the best."

"All right, boys." He turned his attention to the moving men. "Let's see if the two o' youse can handle this one here."

"What's a squat rack?" I said again as we headed for home.

"How do I know. A rack you squat on, I guess," Al said.

"You think we should take him up on it?" I said.

Al shrugged. "Why not. What've we got to lose."

Four

We had tuna casserole for supper that night. Figures. My father was away on a business trip. We never have tuna casserole when he's home.

When I complained, my mother said, "Your father works very hard. He deserves a good dinner."

"That's a very sexist remark," I told her. "You work hard, I work hard. We also deserve a good dinner."

"How about me?" Teddy shouted. "I work hard too. I deserve a good dinner just as much as you guys."

When my mother went out of the room, I said, quietly, "What you deserve, Ted, is a big bowl of dog food. It's chock full of nutrients and vitamins. Plus, it makes fur grow. You eat it, you'll most likely be the furriest kid in the fourth grade."

"Yeah." Teddy drooped all over the table, as boneless as an octopus. "Only if I ate dog food, I'd probably only bark instead of talk."

I looked cross-eyed at him and he barked loudly.

"Bath time, Teddy," my mother said.

Teddy said woof woof to her.

"I bet you have fleas too, don't you, sweetheart?" I whispered. In answer, Teddy wiped his snotty little nose on me and shouted woof woof while shaking himself madly and brushing off tons of fleas onto me.

"I'm calling Hubie!" Teddy cried, racing to the phone. After he barked at Hubie a while, Hubie must've hung up. Teddy banged the receiver down and rolled around, taking bites out of his own arm and barking up a storm.

"You should study to be a bone specialist," I told him. "You have the head for it."

That stopped him cold. His mouth dropped open and I heard the wheels in his head creaking as he tried to figure that one out. I went to my room, filled with the glow that comes from having had the last word.

The telephone rang. My mother got it on the second ring. Maybe it was my father calling, which he sometimes does when he's out of town.

Suddenly I had to go to the bathroom. Doing math does that to me.

"It was Polly," my mother said. "I told her you'd call her back when you finished your homework. She said it was a matter of life and death. I told her to put both of them on hold. She said she'd try Al."

"What'd she want?"

"Oh, she said something about a tea dance. Her cousin or some relative. I'm not sure." Vaguely she waved the crossword puzzle at me. "This one's tough," she said. "A five-letter word for coercion, ending in *y*." She tapped her teeth with her pencil, a sure sign she doesn't know the word. She always saves the puzzle for after supper. She claims her head is at its best then.

I finished my math, fast. Polly's line was busy. So was Al's. I knew it. They were talking to each other.

"I'm just going to Al's for a sec," I told my mother.

My mother frowned at me and from her expression I could tell she was far away. Good. I like her far away sometimes. I escaped.

I knocked twice. Al didn't answer. I knew her mother was out for dinner, so I tried the door. It was unlocked. I slid into Al's apartment.

"I'm here!" I hollered so she wouldn't think I was a burglar.

"She's here," I heard her say. She was on the phone in her mother's bedroom, probably with her shoes off so as not to get the bedspread dirty.

"Yeah," Al said. "I'll ask her. She just got here. She's been running. She looks sort of wild eyed, like someone's been after her. Sure. I'll put her on. You can spring it on her yourself." Al handed me the telephone.

"What's up, Polly?" I said.

The receiver was warm, almost hot. They'd been chewing the fat for a long time.

"I'm sounding you out," Polly said. "My cousin Harry—you know, the one I told you about who's got one blue eye and one brown one—well, he goes to this boys' academy on West Eightieth Street and they're having a tea dance next month and he asked me to fix him up. Harry's sort of shy, you see, and he doesn't know any girls. He has a friend. The friend also wants to be fixed up. So I thought of you and Al."

"What does 'fix up' mean?" I said.

"It means he wants a date," Polly said.

"You mean a blind date?" I said. "Like what we were talking about on Sunday? Is that what you're driving at?"

"Well," said Polly, "I guess you could call it that. If you want."

"What's Harry got going for him besides one blue eye and one brown one?" I asked.

"Not a heck of a lot," Polly said. "Except for his brain. He's supersmart. His board scores are fab. He's fifteen and already a junior. He skipped fifth grade, he was so smart."

"How come you don't go with him to this tea dance?" I said.

"I already asked her that," Al said, pacing around

the rug. "I can't tea-dance. All I can do is disco." And she discoed around, showing a lot of arm motion.

"The thing is," Polly went on, "this tea dance is sponsored every year by the junior class and you can't go if you don't bring a date. Harry's really uptight about it. He's a nice guy, so I said I'd help him out. It only goes from four to six. That's only two hours. You can handle two hours, can't you?"

"I'm not sure," I said. "Two hours can be an eternity. Like when you're in the dentist's chair, for instance."

"Harry's not the dentist, for Pete's sake," Polly said. "He's perfectly O.K. I mean, he's not peculiar or anything. Know what I mean?"

"No," I said.

"Let me talk to her," Al said, hand out for the phone.

"How tall is he?" Al asked Polly.

I put my ear as close to the receiver as I could and heard Polly say, "You already asked me that. I told you he's no midget. He's tall."

"How tall?" Al wouldn't let go. She had a thing about being taller than boys her age. Or older. One thing about Brian, she said. He was tall. He got a little taller every time she told me about him. I figured by now he must be about seven feet. And a great basketball player.

"I don't know exactly." Polly sounded as if she was losing her patience. "You want me to call him up and ask his mother to measure him against the wall?"

"Don't get your knickers twisted," Al said.

"Ask her how tall his friend is," I said.

"How tall's his friend?" Al asked.

"Hey, these guys aren't trying to get into the army, for Pete's sake!" I heard Polly say in a loud voice. "All they want is a date for a lousy tea dance."

"How come you don't go with the friend?" Al said.

I put my ear as close to the telephone as I could, but I couldn't hear what Polly said.

"We'll get back to you," Al said. "We have to discuss the matter. What do you wear to a tea dance anyway? A formal? Heels? A tiara? What?"

Polly let out one of her super-duper Bronx cheers, one that made the rafters ring. Her father had taught her how. He takes Polly to see the Yankees play now and then. Polly has made an in-depth study of how to give a Bronx cheer. She's very good at it.

"Ouch," Al said, holding the receiver away from her ear. "That hurt. All right for you. Next time you call up, I'm putting you on hold."

After she'd hung up, I said, "Does that mean we'd be blind dates?"

"You got me, lieutenant," Al said. "All I know is it's a tea dance and I don't like the sound of that. I don't even like tea. Probably we'd have to slop down gallons of tea and I don't have a tea-dance dress or shoes or a hat. Or gloves." She gave me a shot of her bilious eye. "I have a feeling deep in my heart that when you go to a tea dance, you wear gloves. You know my mother. She's been trying to get me into a pair of white gloves as long as I can remember. I'll tower over him. I know I will. Probably I'll have to dance with him the entire time. Two whole hours. Probably no one will cut in or anything."

"What does that mean?" I asked her.

"When a boy cuts in on you"—Al resumed pacing around the rug, staring at the ceiling—"it means he taps the shoulder of the boy you happen to be dancing with on account of he wants to dance with you himself. Then you change partners." Al took a few deep breaths. She was starting to hyperventilate. She always hyperventilates when she's nervous.

"So, when you're fat and ugly and your hair is full of split ends, and no one wants to dance with you, including the kid you're dancing with"—Al spread her hands wide— "you're stuck with the same guy until the music stops.

"My mother told me that when she was young she always used to be cut in on quite a lot. She always tells me stuff like that. I wish she wouldn't," Al said.

"Why?" I said.

"Because I don't want to know if she was cut in on and she was popular and all that junk," Al said. "It makes me feel bad because she wants me to be cut in on and popular too and I won't. Ever. Be popular, that is."

"Don't be a ninny," I told her. "You will too. Remember what Mr. Richards said. He said we'd both be stunners someday. He knew what he was talking about. He was a very wise man. Hang in there."

"Listen." Al turned to me and her face was fierce. "Who cares. Look at it this way. The kid's fifteen and already a junior. He doesn't know any girls to ask to his tea dance, so he has to get his cousin to scrounge up a couple. That means he's no hotshot or anything, right? No big deal."

"You're absolutely right," I said.

"And what's more," Al said, very glum, "probably he could be Napoleon in my epic poem when they make it into a movie on account of he's the same size as Napoleon, which I happen to know is about five feet two inches tall."

"I thought that role was going to Michael J. Fox," I reminded her.

"Oh, it is, it is," Al said. "But in case Michael J. has a bellyache or some other malady, this tea-dance guy, who is so short he only comes up to my sternum, could step into the role in a trice. He's Napoleonesque, as they say."

"Napoleon as a teenager, that is," I said.

"Yeah. You got it. Napoleon as a teenager," Al said. "And we all know nobody ever cut in on him, right?"

Five

The next morning I opened the apartment door and almost fell over Al. She was leaning against the wall, staring down at her feet.

She stuck one of her legs out, with the foot pointing like an arrow straight at me.

"Whaddaya think?" she said. "I'm not sure they're me." She made a face. "The real me, that is."

"They aren't anyone," I said, glad she'd asked. Those shoes were plenty grotty, all right. They reminded me of witch shoes, long and flat, with nerdy little heels.

"Gunboats," Al said glumly. "Big black gunboats. Why does she buy me shoes anyway? They're my feet, aren't they? I'm entitled to pick out my own shoes. If I bought shoes for her, she'd have a cow. And my toe's right up to the end already. I can be crippled for life if I wear these babies."

Al's mother buys her stuff at the store where she's in Better Dresses on account of she gets a twenty percent employee discount. Some of the things she buys Al loves, like her lavender sweater. Others she hates.

Al buzzed for the elevator, still staring at her feet. Shoes can do that to you, the wrong shoes, I mean. The elevator bounced to a stop and the door creaked open. The woman from the top floor stood there with her miserable little dog that thinks he owns the world. He had these tiny little eyes and a nose you can look up, if you're close enough and you stomach can handle it, and see all the way inside his head. He looks as if he's wearing a body wig. Plus, he smells. He is a totally disgusting little dog. Sometimes he's on a leash, sometimes she drapes him over her shoulder, giving him little pats as if he was a baby and she's burping him. Today he was nestled on her neck like a live fur piece, looking at us with his tiny eyes filled with hostility. The tip of his tiny tongue stuck out of his mouth, and you can't tell me he wasn't sticking his tongue out at us. He was like one of those wizened little heads people bring back from the rain forests of Brazil.

"Hello," we said, skinning to the back of the car. The woman inclined her head slightly, just barely acknowledging our existence. She had on a black-and-white polka-dotted raincoat and a hat to match, although there wasn't a drop of rain in sight. She always wears black lipstick and her cheekbones are hollowed out with brown blush. I think she's in the cosmetics business. She looks to me like the kind of person who's never been a child. Probably back when she was our age, they didn't have teenagers. My father says teenagers hadn't been invented yet when he was a boy.

You have to take what my father says with a grain of salt, however. Behind the woman's back we made faces at her dog. Al put her thumbs in her ears and waggled her fingers at him, and I pushed up my nose and pulled my eyes down. The dog's eyes rolled wildly and he snorted at us.

"What's his name?" Al asked in her phony sweetsy voice.

"Sparky," the woman said. At the sound of his name, Sparky thrashed around, letting out a series of nervous little farts. Al held her nose and I fought the giggle attack I could feel building inside me. I swallowed hard and the giggles receded.

Sparky's mom put him down on the floor, and Sparky sniffed at our ankles and heaved daintily.

Al tapped the woman on the shoulder and said, "I think your dog's going to be sick."

"Oh, he never gets sick," Sparky's mom said with great conviction, not even turning to look. Whereupon

Sparky let fly. All over one of Al's new shoes. She jabbed an elbow into my ribs, red faced, not wanting me to miss anything. It wasn't a big barf, as Sparky was a very small dog, but it was a barf nevertheless. We laughed nervously. Al didn't seem to mind about the barf hitting her new shoe. In fact, she perked up considerably.

"Whoa, Sparky," Al said as Sparky finished barfing and began to pee on her other new shoe.

In a stage whisper, Al said, "Sparky peed on my shoe." The woman stared straight ahead. Sparky shook himself triumphantly and his long hair flew every which way as he rearranged his little self after the unexpected flurry of activity. The elevator thudded to a stop, and when the door opened Sparky's mom whisked Sparky out so fast his little feet skimmed the floor.

"They're ruined," Al said happily, showing me her shoes in the harsh light of day. "Look. They'll never be the same. I can't wear them ever, ever again." And she did a couple of bumps and grinds to celebrate.

"Here," I said, handing her a tissue. "You might be able to save 'em if you wipe 'em off right away. They'll be good as new. All I can say is, I'm glad your mother didn't pay full price for those little beauties."

"Please." Al held up her hand. "God sent Sparky to me because I'm a good person. Sparky had a mission in life, which was to louse up these shoes. I must think of a suitable reward."

"How about a one-way ticket on the Staten Island ferry?" I said.

"Or perhaps a gift certificate for the Chic Chien," Al suggested.

We wandered toward school, both of us in a good mood.

"Why do you suppose she named him Sparky?" I said.

"Probably because her boyfriend gave him to her and he's an auto mechanic," Al said.

"Yeah, and Sparky bears a strong resemblance to a spark plug, right?"

"Yeah, and the best part's when she looks up Sparky's nose," Al said. "It reminds her of her boy-friend."

"Gross!" I said. We both got a little hysterical. Actually, for a day that had started out plenty zilchy, it was turning out pretty well.

When we got to school the bell was about to ring. We watched Mr. Keogh break up a fight outside the boys' room. Mr. Keogh used to be our homeroom teacher. He used to call Al Al, but ever since he took us to the Bronx to visit his father in the old-people's home, and Al did her Mother Zandi fortune-telling routine, he calls Al Mother Zandi.

"How's business, Mother Zandi?" Mr. Keogh asked Al, straightening his bow tie.

"Not a heck of a lot going on right now, Mr. Keogh,"

Al replied. "It's our slow season. How's your father doing?"

"About the same. Sometimes he knows me, sometimes not." Mr. Keogh looked sad. "The doctors say that's the way it'll be with him. Some bright days, some dark. My father's a good man. It seems to me he deserves better."

We agreed, and I thought that my father deserved better too. I can't imagine my father ever being in an old-people's home and made up my mind then and there that I'd never let that happen to him.

To cheer Mr. Keogh up, we told him about Sparky and Al's new shoes.

Mr. Keogh laughed so hard tears came to his eyes. He had to take out his handkerchief and blow his nose and wipe his eyes before he could go back to class.

"I'm glad I ran into you two," he told us. "You're always good for a laugh."

"A good laugh is good for the soul," we said in unison.

"Right you are, girls. And my soul needed a laugh in the worst way," Mr. Keogh said. "Thanks." And he walked away.

"Mr. Keogh is very spry for a man of forty-one," Al told me.

"Mr. Richards was very spry for a man of advanced years too," I said. "And he was right when he said a good laugh is good for the soul."

"He usually was," Al said. "Right, that is."

"Did you tell your mother about the free tryout at Al's Health Club?" I asked her.

"No," Al said. "I figure what she don't know don't hurt her, et cetera. What I say is let's just go for it. Did you tell yours?"

"No," I said. "I figure likewise."

Six

The idea came into my head without warning; full blown, perfect, beautiful. Why not ask Ms. Bolton if she'd like to come to Al's Health Club for a free tryout? Nothing like a good workout to get your mind off your problems, I always say.

No sooner had the thought occurred to me than I heard Al's special ring: two, then one, then two.

"It's Al!" Teddy roared, beating me to the door against all odds. I stuck out my left foot, which is bigger than the right one, and he soared over it like an Olympic champion.

"You can't come in!" he shouted, flinging the door open. "We're quarantined!" A kid in Teddy's class had the mumps and the doctor said he was quarantined until he got over the contagious part. Teddy was mad with jealousy. He longed to be quarantined too.

"Get lost, buster," I said, shoving him aside. "Come on, Al. We need our privacy. I've got something very important to discuss."

"Yeah," she said, "me too." Then Teddy leaped on her, hoping to wrestle her to the ground. But she was too strong for him. She got his head in a tight grip and he was powerless.

"Slap me five, bro," Al said when at last she freed Teddy. "How's it going, o prince of the realm? What's happening, man? How's things up in the nutmeg state, as we aficionados call it?"

It blows Teddy's mind when Al talks that way. She might as well be talking in tongues, but he eats it up.

Teddy visits our cousins up in Connecticut a lot. When he comes home he's more impossible than when he left. The things that go on up there, Teddy tells us, shaking his head despairingly, are beyond belief. He hints at all kinds of outrageous events. I guess the kids up there figure Teddy's the big cheese from the Big Apple and probably spends most of his time hanging out in massage parlors and checking out the porno films in Time Square.

"We saw some Mafia guys this time," Teddy told Al. He's got a thing about every second person in Connecticut being a Mafia guy.

"We were standing in line at the movies," Teddy

went on. "And they were right ahead of us. They were real stuff, all right."

"How'd you know?" Al asked.

"On account of the lumps," Teddy said.

"The lumps," Al said.

"Yeah. That's how you tell they're Mafia guys," Teddy said. "They got these lumps under their jackets. That's the tip-off."

"What kind of lumps?" Al wanted to know.

"Rods," Teddy said, softly so my mother wouldn't hear. "Guns. They pack their rods in holsters under their jackets in case they get ambushed. There's lots of people trying to rub 'em out. They have a price on their heads. That's what my cousin Craig says and it's true."

Craig's eleven. He calls all the shots. What he says is what Teddy believes.

"Come on," I said, pulling Al toward my room. "We haven't got all night."

We heard my mother coming. Teddy jumped as if he'd been stung by a wasp and hid behind the curtains. "Shhh," he said, finger to lips. "Don't tell her. If she knew she wouldn't let me go there any-more."

"Why, hello, Al," my mother said. "I didn't hear you come in. I saw your mother in the elevator the other day and I couldn't get over how well she looks. You'd never even know she'd been sick."

"Yeah, the doctor says she's in good shape," Al said.

"But she still has to take it easy. I make sure she eats the right foods and gets plenty of rest."

"You sound like a TV commercial," I told her.

Al's mother had to go to the hospital this summer with pneumonia. Al called off her plans to go to a barn dance at her father's farm to stay with her mother. She wanted to go in the worst way, but she said her mother wouldn't walk out on her if she had pneumonia. They were going to have home-made ice cream and Brian was going to be there. Al's father and Louise, her stepmother, sent Al a T-shirt with AL(exandra) THE GREAT on it to show her how they felt about her. She loves that T-shirt so much that sometimes she wears it to bed.

Out of the corner of my eye I saw Teddy peering furtively from behind the curtains, waiting for my mother to split.

"One last warning, Teddy," my mother said briskly. "Clean up your room. I won't say it again," and she sailed out of the room like a ship under full sail.

"Come on," I said to Al again.

"I wanna hear too," Teddy sniveled.

"This is top-level stuff, Ted," Al said. "It's only in the planning stage. When we get to liftoff time, we'll let you in on it."

Teddy bought that and we zipped into my room and locked the door.

Al smiled and said in her deep, dark, swami voice, "It is ordained. Ms. Bolton goes to health club, tightens bod to gorgeous, meets fab billionaire, sweeps him off his feet. After knot is tied, Ms. Bolton rewards us for turning her life around, hands over keys to limo, Tiffany charge card, fur coats and diamonds for distribution to the poor. Peels off roll of C notes, says 'Do with these what you will.' "

"Names first kid after me," I said, getting into it, "and second after you."

Trust Al. I plug around at my usual turtle trot and she's already mapping out Ms. Bolton's exotic new life.

Outside the locked door, Teddy scratched and barked, wanting in.

"You got a dog?" Al said, surprised.

"Yeah. A rottweiler named Boris," I said. "He looks fierce, but he's a real pussy cat."

"I'd love a dog but my mother says nix," Al said. She took one look at Teddy on all fours and said, "Looks more like a poodle than a rottweiler to me."

Teddy woofed woofed and Al patted him on the head.

"Keep the burglars out, Ted," she told him. "I have to split." We went to the door.

"Know what?" Al said halfway down the hall. "I say we give the roll of C notes to the homeless. Like that woman with her hand out."

We'd seen a desperate-looking woman begging last month. Al had gone back several times to the place we'd seen her and tried to find her, but neither of us ever saw her again. There were lots of women who looked like her, but Al wanted to find that one and give her money.

"I'm serious," Al said.

"Hey, it's a gag," I said. "There is no roll of C notes. Don't you remember? You made it all up. It was all in fun."

Al was at the door, opening it with the key she wore on a string around her neck. She used that key even when her mother was inside, she'd got so used to it.

She raised a finger and said, "Mother Zandi says it will come true."

I nodded. When Al gets intense, the best thing is to stay cool.

"Have a weird day, comrade," she said, and went inside.

Seven

"Did your mother have a cow?" I asked Al as we dawdled our way to school the next morning.

"About what?" She seemed preoccupied.

"Your new shoes," I said. "Sparky's revenge."

"Oh, I tossed 'em into the back of my closet," she said. "Let 'em simmer some; then when they start fouling up the joint, she can search and destroy. If there's anything that bugs my mother, it's bad smells. She uses room deodorizer at the drop of a hat. Do you want to ask her or shall I?"

We were back to Ms. Bolton.

"I don't care," I said, which wasn't strictly true. I did care.

"How about if we toss a coin?" I said.

Al looked at me, her face closed and bleak.

"You know what I dreamed last night?" she said.

"You dreamed about the woman we saw with the sign that said, PLEASE HELP ME," I said. Al's mouth dropped open. "You dreamed she spoke to you or something," I went on, flushed with success, knowing I'd hit the nail on the head. "Maybe she spit at you or something like that."

"How did you know?" Al asked me.

"From the expression on your face," I said. "Besides, we were talking about her. She's on your conscience. If it'll make you feel better, we could go back again to where we saw her and look for her. Only trouble is, I don't have any money. For her, I mean. I'm flat broke."

"Neither do I," Al said somberly. "I spent it all. On candy, and I gave the rest to the blind man on Fifth Avenue. You want to know how much the candy cost and how much I gave the blind man?"

"No," I said.

It started to rain. We ran for it. Even so, we got wet. I looked at myself in the mirror in the girl's room. My hair was plastered all over my face like a camouflage net. My own mother wouldn't know me. Al went to the toilet.

"Know something?" she called to me as I ran my fingers through my hair to make it look better. "I've been thinking about the tea dance. I'm not going. Even if he does have one blue eye and one brown one. I'm not galumphing around at a tea dance with a totally wonky-eyed stranger, even if he is Polly's cousin."

"Suit yourself," I said. If she thought I was going to coax her, she had another think coming.

The water roared and Al came out and washed her hands for about five minutes, frowning down at them as she did so.

"Come on," I said finally. I was getting itchy. "You got all the germs off. They're flopping around breathing their last. Let's go."

Al dried her hands slowly on a paper towel. "The thing of it is," she said, "I want to go but I don't want to. Savvy? I mean, I'd have to force myself to go. If I went, which I very much doubt, I'd have to make myself go. It'd be a new experience and Lord knows at my age I need all the new experiences I can get. But it'd probably turn out to be a bummer. A real bummer. Probably he'd say hi and I'd say hi and that'd be it for the dialogue. I mean, what does this dude go for? Is he into sports or music or art or what? Does he like to read, or is he a TV person? If he thinks I'm just gonna sit there and smile and ask him what his interests are, he can just take a hike. He has to find out what *my* interests are, what kind of a person I am. I'm not putting up with any chauvinism. No way."

"Cool it," I said. "First things first. Let's get things squared away with Ms. Bolton. Now."

She was at her desk, marking papers. Somewhat stealthily, we snuck up on her.

"You go," I mouthed. Al mouthed back, "No, you."

"Ms. Bolton," I began.

"We wondered if . . ." Al said at the same time.

We laughed nervously.

"What can I do for you?" Ms. Bolton asked us.

"We're going to a health club for a free tryout." I spoke very fast. "Want to come with us?"

"We're tightening up our bods," Al said, also speaking fast, "and we thought you might like to tighten yours too." Then, realizing how that sounded, she turned a fiery red.

Ms. Bolton seemed to be trying not to laugh. "That's very nice," she said. "I used to work out a lot. At home. I haven't done anything like that in the city. A free tryout, huh? That's a first. You sure it's all right for me to come along? Maybe you'd better check first."

"Oh, I'm sure it's all right," I said. "This guy's got a new place and he's anxious to get customers. It's only for an hour. Then he figures we go home and spread the word about how great the place is."

"Well . . ." Ms. Bolton hesitated. "It sounds real nice. And you're real nice to think of me. When did you plan on going?"

"Tomorrow?" Al and I looked at each other.

"I have to get a leotard," I said. "That's what you're supposed to wear, isn't it? A leotard."

"I'm not wearing any leotard," Al said, looking

alarmed. "If you think I'm shoving myself into one of those babies, you're nuts. I'm wearing sweat pants."

"Sure. Anything goes. Whatever you're comfortable in," Ms. Bolton said. "Tell you what. I'll bring my stuff with me tomorrow and if it suits, fine. If not, that's O.K. too."

The bell rang.

"Thanks, kids. I really appreciate it," Ms. Bolton said.

After school we set out for Al's Health Club to check things out.

"She really has great bone structure," Al said.

"Who?"

"Ms. Bolton, dummy. Bone structure is very important. I have lousy bone structure. My bones are lost in my pudge."

"There's no such word as *pudge*," I said.

"That's what you think. I just invented it," Al said.

"Have it your way."

Between Lexington and Third Avenue we saw two people sleeping in doorways. They were surrounded by bulging shopping bags and, although it was a warm, pleasant fall day, they seemed to be wearing several layers of clothing. Neither one stirred as we passed.

"I read in the paper they'd rather live on the streets than go to the shelters," Al said. "On account of the shelters smell so bad and all night long people moan and make terrible noises. A woman reporter spent a couple nights in one of those shelters and said they must be like Bedlam. That's what they called an insane asylum in England long ago. She said it was the worst thing she'd ever experienced. She said it was indescribable, it was so foul."

She didn't expect a reply, so she didn't get one. We walked to the health club thinking our own thoughts. Probably if a panhandler had approached us right at that moment and asked us for money, Al would've given him her Swatch watch on the spot. She loved that watch. It kept perfect time, she said.

The health club looked deserted, although the door was open. There were two men inside, watching TV.

"Come on," Al said, pushing me ahead of her.

"Yeah? Something we can do for you?" One of the men said, not taking his eyes from the screen. It was a game show. People were hollering and hugging each other and crying tears of joy. Someone had won a refrigerator. Or maybe a microwave.

"Is Al here?" I said.

The other man, the handsome one, looked at us. He was handsome in a sort of unhealthy way. His muscles were taut and his body shirt bulged in all the right places. He had all the muscles they mention in the ads: the pecs, the abs, and the gluts. I'm not sure which was which, but I know they're the ones that count.

"Who wants to know?" he said.

Behind me, Al was breathing heavily. This guy

made her mad. I could tell. He was very rude. I've noticed that people are frequently rude to kids but not to adults. For some reason they figure kids don't deserve manners. Maybe that's why a lot of kids don't have any.

"We talked to him a few days ago," Al said in a loud voice. "He said to come back today." I was glad she left out the freebie part.

"Come back tomorrow," the handsome one said. "Al oughta be here tomorrow. And if he's not, you can come back the day after tomorrow. How does that grab you?"

He turned the volume up on the TV. A man in a green shirt was dancing with a woman in a blue-and-white dress. The audience was roaring.

We turned to leave.

At a safe distance, Al shouted, "Who's winning, guys, the Yanks or the Mets?" Then she shoved me and hissed, "Blast off!" and we ran until we both had pains in our sides. Twice we slowed to see whether they were chasing us.

"I think the whole thing's a scam," Al said. "Probably Al's the janitor or something and he doesn't know squat about health clubs. Probably he's a shill and gets a commission on every customer he brings in."

"No," I said. "Al's all right. He had a very sincere face."

"You," Al said scornfully. "Either they've got nice legs or sincere faces. I wouldn't be surprised if those guys were both crooks and they'd knock their grand-mother down the stairs in her wheelchair for a piece of the action."

"You are very cynical," I said.

"Who needs it?" Al snapped. "If we wait long enough, tight bods will be out and loose bods will be in. It's all a matter of timing."

"I think Ms. Bolton really wanted to go," I said. "It was a good idea. We gave it our best shot, anyway."

"Yeah," Al said, stomping along beside me. "Now we'll have to think of something else."

Eight

"I'm out of milk," my mother said when I got home. "Be a good child and nip down to the store and get some. Please."

I groaned. I was beat. But if I told her that, she'd want to know why. I took the money and went.

As luck would have it, Sparky and his mom were coming in just as I was going out.

"Just the person I wanted to see!" Sparky's mom trilled. I backed off. She'd never been the least bit friendly before. Why now?

"I'm in a hurry," I said. "My mother needs some milk pronto."

"This won't take a sec," Sparky's mom said, resting her hand on my arm. Sparky lifted his little lip and sneered at me. He's a very jealous, insecure dog, I realized, unwilling to share his mom's attention. What Sparky needed was a little brother or sister, I thought.

Some of my best thoughts I keep to myself.

"My nephew is visiting me this weekend," Sparky's mom said. "He's a simply darling boy. Brilliant." She rolled her eyes to emphasize how brilliant he was. "His folks are brilliant too. My sister, his mother, had the brains in our family. But I was the good-looking one and I got all the boys!" She crinkled up her nose and looked from side to side to see if she had an audience.

"I really have to go," I said, edging toward the door.

"Will you and your friend, the heavy-set girl, come on Saturday for a small party?" Sparky's mom said. "I'm introducing my nephew to my friends and I thought you two would be just the right age." She narrowed her eyes to slits and leaned close to me as if she was checking to see how old I was. I realized she probably needed glasses and was too vain to wear them. I've seen women in the supermarket with their faces all scrunched and their eyes almost closed, trying to figure out what it was in the packages they were buying. I've never seen any men doing that, only women. That's strange but true.

"My friend?" I said stupidly. If Al ever heard herself described as heavy set she'd freak, totally and absolutely.

"The girl you're always with. I think her name begins with an *A*," said Sparky's mom.

I waited, unwillingly to give her Al's name.

"What is that child's name anyway?" Sparky's mom said.

"We call her Mother Zandi," I said. "She tells fortunes."

"How very peculiar," Sparky's mom said. "She tells fortunes, you say. Oh, I've got it!" and she snapped her fingers. "Allison. That's it, Allison."

"Her real name is Alexandra," I said, "but we call her Al."

"I knew it began with an *A*!" Sparky's mom cried. "Of course. Grand. Would you ask Alexandra if she'd like to join us on Saturday? I'd love it if you'd both come. We'll have loads of refreshments and I just know you two and Josh will hit it off. You'll be crazy about each other. Then you people could go off somewhere to dance or whatever takes your fancy. Dance, perhaps. You do dance, don't you? Disco. That's it, disco, isn't it? All that thrashing around and the music so loud it addles the brains, but still, it's the style. One has to go with what's in style, doesn't one? Never mind. You could all go out on a date and that would be divine. Wouldn't it be divine?"

A date, I thought. A blind date. Al and I were in demand. Our date books would soon be full up. First a tea dance, now this. I got very tired just thinking about it all.

"I'll have to ask my mother," I said, the total nerd.

"Well, of course you will. Would you like me to call her, explain about the party and all?"

"No," I said hastily. The last thing in the world I wanted was for Sparky's mom to call my mom.

"I'll let you know," I said.

When I got back with the milk, my mother was on the telephone. She was talking to her sister up in Connecticut, my aunt Tess. Tess' husband had left her for another woman and she was plenty bitter.

Perfect. I put the milk in the refrigerator and zipped down the hall to Al's. My mother would be good for at least half an hour talking to Tess.

"Enter, infidel!" Al threw open the door. She had on her AL(exandra) T-shirt, her sweat pants, and her red shoes. Plus she had a scarf tied around her head.

"How's this?" she asked, turning so I could get the total affect. "Good, huh? Just right for the Nautilus machine. I'm trying the roto curl bar first, then I'm going for the leg press and the super pullover. I'm all set."

"You better bag the shoes," I told her. "They'll

never let you in with those beauties on. And what's with the headdress? You been doing the windows or something?"

"This is my wimple," Al said, very dignified.

"And a wimple's what a wimp wears, right?" I thought that was pretty funny, but Al didn't crack a smile.

"You jest," she said. "I, Mother Zandi, am searching for my past and future self. I have placed myself back in time. I see myself as I was in my life before this one."

"And that's when you wore your wimple," I said.

Al inclined her head. I think that meant yes.

"In ancient times"—Al made her voice very deep— "I was a woman in the Temple of Dendur. I had a white cat. I was thought to be a witch. In those days, all witches had white cats. It was a rule."

"Maybe instead of being a woman in the Temple of Dendur," I said, "you were a white cat."

"Hey!" Al snapped out of her Mother Zandi persona. "Neat. Very good. I like that. O.K., so I was a white cat in the Temple of Dendur. Creeping about listening, hearing all secrets, telling none. White cats were thought to be messengers of Satan. I think it was Satan. Or was that black cats. Anyway, you get the picture. What are you here for, o messenger of the gods? What news bringeth thee for me?"

"You'll never guess," I said. "We, thee and me, are

invited to a party by Sparky's mom. What thinketh you of thateth?"

"Holy Toledo, don't tell me she's throwing a birthday bash for the little bugger," Al said. "I can't stand it."

"Nope. She's throwing a bash for her nephew, who's not only brilliant, he's also a darling boy and he's coming to visit her this weekend."

"She wants both of us?" Al said. "And there's only one nephew. How come?"

"She says after the refreshments if we hit it off the way she thinks we will, we can go discoing."

"You know what this is," Al said. "This is a blind date, pure and simple. She sets us up, we never laid eyes on each other before, we hit it off, we go on a date. Awesome."

I nodded.

Dramatically, Al stripped off her wimple and stepped out of her red shoes.

"Excuse me," she said. "I have to go to the bathroom."

I sat there, thinking about the meaning of life. Of being popular. Of blind dates. Of what the heck this was all about.

Al returned.

"Are you up for it?" she asked me.

"If you are," I said.

"How tall is he?"

"I don't know. Maybe we better call her up and ask."

"What's Sparky's mom's name?" Al wanted to know.

"I don't know," I said again. "I always call her Sparky's mom."

"You think she'd be listed in the phone book that way?" Al said.

Nine

My mother would know. She always knows things like people's last names, how many times they've been married, how many kids they've had, where the money comes from. Minutiae, I believe it's called.

"What's the name of that woman on the top floor?" I asked her, casual as heck, peeling potatoes like a pro. "The one with the scroungy little dog."

My mother was making pie crust and didn't answer. I thought she hadn't heard, although as I said, her hearing's first rate. She doesn't miss a cough or a sneeze, even if it's midnight and I have a pillow over my face. She never misses the sound of the top of the cookie jar being lifted by experts, which I consider myself and which Teddy certainly is.

"Out of there!" she hollers. "It's almost dinnertime. You'll spoil your appetite." One of the things I look forward to about growing up and moving out is not having my mother's ears around. I know I'll miss her like crazy, but the ears I can do without.

"There," she said, putting the final crimp on the crust.

"Her name's Mrs. Olmstead. He was president of a copper company and the money's his. Third husband, I believe. No children." My mother brushed the top of the crust with egg white to give it a professional glaze.

"Now she raises funds. Sells tickets for benefits to all her friends, gets the right people to take a table at a charity ball. That sort of thing. She used to be vice-president of a fragrance company. In everyday language, kid, that's perfume. She's not friendly. We've been in the building almost ten years and I think she's said hello twice. I can take her or leave her." My mother opened the oven and shoved the pie in.

"Why?"

Just when I'm sure she's lost the train of thought, she zeros in. She kills me. She really does.

"She invited me and Al to a party she's giving for her nephew," I said. "She's having lots of young people and refreshments."

"Well, for pity's sake." My mother looked at me

with something like admiration. At least, I think that's what it was.

"What did you do to get in her good graces? Or what did Al do? I'm flabbergasted. Flummoxed, you might even say," my mother said.

"Well," I said, wondering if I could trust my mother not to tell Al's mother. "Sparky ruined Al's new shoe, you see." I told her about the barf and the pee and how delighted Al was that her shoe was ruined on account of she'd hated those shoes that her mother bought her.

"So Al's kind of grateful to the mutt," I explained. "Even if he is sort of repulsive."

"He's all of that," my mother agreed. "Imagine being cooped up with that face all day. Imagine having to take him to the park, where he has to be followed around with one of those dreadful pooper scoopers. Imagine having to scoop up his poop. I'd be embarrassed to be seen scooping up my dog's poop."

I burst out laughing. "You looked so funny when you said that!" I said. "You cross your heart and hope to die you won't tell Al's mother, though. She might get mad."

"What do you take me for, a squealer?" my mother said indignantly. "I won't say a word, though I do think Mrs. Olmstead ought to at least offer to get Al's shoe cleaned. Are you going to her party, you and Al?"

"I said I'd let her know," I said. "I wasn't sure you'd let me."

"Of course I'll let you," my mother said. "It's only upstairs. If the nephew turns out to be a bummer, come on down. Besides, I'd like to know what her apartment is like. She had it decorated last year by one of the top New York designers. I understand it cost the earth. So keep your eyes peeled. I think she has silk walls in the drawing room and her dining room is black."

My mother set her mouth in that way that she has when she disapproves strongly of something.

"A black dining room is not good form, it seems to me," she said, pressing her lips into a thin line. "What's the nephew like, did she say?"

"She said he was brilliant and a darling boy," I said.

My mother clapped a hand to her forehead. "Oh-oh," she said. "Beware of brilliant darling boys. How old is he?"

"I didn't ask," I said.

"How tall is he, then?"

"I didn't ask that either. You sound just like Al. She always thinks boys are going to be midgets, that they're going to come up to her sternum or her belly button or something. She has a thing about it."

"That's because she's tall," my mother said. "I was always tall for my age too. And for some inexplicable reason, the short boys went for me straight away and all the tall boys seemed to prefer the short girls. Unfair, but that's the way it was. I know how Al feels."

I'd never thought of it until that minute. How tall was Brian? Al had never told me. All she talked about was Brian's big muscles and how he made the city boys look like Charlie Brown.

"Mom," I said, "did you ever go on a blind date?"

"Why, I was the blind-date queen of the eighth grade," my mother said proudly. "In that grade alone, I had three blind dates. Each one was with the brother of a friend who needed a date in the worst way and couldn't get one. One of my friends charged her brother fifty cents when I said I'd go to the dance with him. It was a finder's fee, she said. He put up a good fight, but in the end he paid her, and afterward she told me she should've charged him a buck. I thought I was worth at least a buck. Maybe more."

"Was it fun? Did you have a good time?" I asked her.

"No," she said. "I can't honestly say it was fun. We were both too uptight. But I'd never been on a date and I felt I was ready to get my feet wet. We didn't have a single thing in common. He was bored and so was I. He'd been to dancing school, so he knew how to dance. I'd been to dancing school too, but I wasn't a very good dancer. He left me to dance with a girl in a pink dress. Her name was Felicia. Oh, how I hated her. I could hardly wait for the evening to end. Then there was the business of what I should do if he tried to kiss me. That kept me awake nights. You see, in those days," my mother said, giving me a piercer, "a kiss was a big deal." She fell silent and had a little smile on her face. I guess she was thinking about those olden days of her youth.

"Did he try?" I asked. I didn't want to seem too eager. All I wanted was for her to go on and on, leaving nothing out.

"I think he did," she said. "Remember, this was long ago. He sort of lunged at me and almost knocked me off our front steps. I lunged the other way and we missed contact by a good five feet. And when I went in, there was Tess, sitting on the living-room couch in her nightgown, pretending to read a book. She was waiting up for me because our parents had gone to the movies or something. 'What happened?' she asked me. I can still see her, wide eyed, wanting some tale of wild events, so, of course, I made some up. I went all out, until Tess' eyes were so wide I could see myself in them as if they were a mirror. That was the best part of the evening, telling Tess my version of what hadn't happened."

My mother laughed at the memory.

"Oh, Mom," I said. "I wish I'd known you when you were young."

"Yes," my mother said. "Just think. You might've

been the friend whose brother I went to the dance with for a fifty-cent finder's fee."

"You'd never go out with Teddy!" I said, shocked. "Not in a million years."

Ten

The next morning Al and I skinned down the service stairs instead of waiting for the elevator. We didn't want to take the chance of running into Sparky's mom. We still hadn't decided whether we'd take her up on her invite.

"What's that?" I pointed to Al's book bag, which was stuffed with what looked like a bunch of old clothes.

"My sweats," Al said. "I figured we might give the health club another shot on our way home. After all, Al did seem a kindly gentleman." She gave me her owl eye for an instant. "So I'm prepared. How about you?"

"My leotard's too small," I said. "I tried it on last night. It's about right for Teddy, I figure."

"Hey, cool," Al said. "Teddy as a ballet dancer. It boggles the mind, *n'est-ce pas?* If Ted decides he wants to emulate Barishnykov, he can save your folks a bundle by skipping into your leotard and they won't have to buy him a new one."

"I had a discussion with my mother last night about blind dates," I said. "She had three blind dates in the eighth grade. All with friends' brothers. She said she had a lousy time."

"No kidding? I asked my mother if she'd ever gone on a blind date and you know what she said?"

"No. What?"

"She said her mother was very, very strict, so strict my mother couldn't even go out with a boy unless she brought the boy home so her mother could meet him, check him out and all. How do you like them apples?"

"That's strict, all right," I agreed. "My mother said she was always taller than the boys her age. She said the short boys always picked her to dance with."

"I knew your mother and I had lots in common!" Al said, smiling. "I appreciate her predicament. I bet if Michael J. Fox and I were at the same dance, he'd make a beeline for me when they played a waltz. Same with R. Redford. I hear he also goes for the tall ones. If that happened, all the other girls would be green with envy, I bet."

"How tall is Brian?" I said. "You never told me."

"Oh, he's tall," Al said. "Pretty tall. He's still growing, of course. Guys reach their full growth a lot later than girls do, you know. Ask any medical doctor, they'll tell you.

"I just wondered," I said. "I mean, you're always asking how tall some boy is and you never told me how tall Brian is, so all I'm doing is asking."

"Next time I write him, I'll ask him," Al said. I knew she was being sarcastic, but I said, "Yeah, good idea," anyway.

"What'll we do about Sparky's mom's fête?" Al said. "We can't go on dodging her. My heart won't take the strain of taking the stairs every time we go in or out of the building. It's crazy. What if we run into her in the elevator and she pins us up to the mat and says 'Gimme a yes or a no.' What then?"

"She'll probably sic Sparky on us," I said. "The mutt will start in on our feet and nibble his way up."

"I tell you one thing," Al said. "If that mutt sinks one fang into me, I'll give him such a case of indigestion he'll never touch another bite of girl again as long as he lives. He'll barf and pee and heave up such a storm his little insides will rumble for weeks."

"You are really and truly gross," I said. I love it when Al's gross. She lets her imagination soar when it comes to being gross. It's part of her charm.

"What I want to know is what do we do about Polly's cousin and the tea dance," I said. "If we don't go, Polly might get sore."

"Does that mean she'll cut off the invites to join her for Sunday lunch and other goodies?" Al said.

"Probably."

"Then I tell you what. You go," Al said, "and I'll stay home with a good book." And although we'd been fooling around, I knew she was serious.

"You mean go without you?" I said.

"Sure. You're much more the thé dansant type than I am," Al said. "I can see you now, spinning around the dance floor, one hand on your partner's shoulder, the other clutching a cup of tea. You go and tell me how it went. I'd be like a bull in a china shop at a tea dance."

"You would not," I said. "That's crazy."

"Yes, I would. Believe me, I know my own limitations. Hey"—Al was suddenly jolly, changing the subject—"let's ask Ms. Bolton is she wants to go to the health club today. I brought my sweats and you can wear your gym shorts. They'd be perfect."

I got mad.

"Why do you always have to go and spoil things?" I said. "We always do things together. I don't want to go to the tea dance without you. Part of the fun is going together. You know that."

Al was silent. Then she said, "Have you wondered why all of a sudden we're in demand? Everyone wants us for tea dances and fêtes for brilliant, darling nephews. Only we're in demand by people who've never seen us. Polly's cousin hasn't seen us, and anyway,

74

what does he know with one blue eye and one brown. And Sparky's mom has never really seen us because she's too vain to wear glasses, without which she's practically blind. If Sparky's mom could see us as we are, our true selves, she'd dump us fast. All of the above is true. The God's truth. Respectfully, signed Mother Zandi."

"O.K.," I said, after thinking about what she'd said. "My gym shorts are dirty but who cares. Let's go. A good workout is good for the bones."

Al scrooched up her face and said, "Did Mr. Richards say that?"

"No," I said. "I did."

Eleven

Ms. Bolton was game. Luckily, she had her workout gear stowed in her tote bag. We arranged to meet out front after last bell. Al and I were pretty excited. All of a sudden, it seemed a pretty daring thing to ask your teacher to go to a health club for a free tryout.

"I sure hope she likes it," Al kept saying.

"How about us?" I said. "Don't you hope we like it too?"

"We're kids. We like practically anything," Al said. "Grownups, especially teachers, are harder to please."

We got our English papers back. Martha Moseley

got an A minus and there was a minute there when I thought she might possibly blow her brains out.

"How can this *be*?" Martha said. "How *can* this be?"

I got a C. Al got a C plus. Ms. Bolton had written across the top of my paper, "Lacks focus!" Al's was crisscrossed with Ms. Bolton's red-pencil corrections of Al's spelling and punctuation.

"Are you sure this is a good idea?" Al said at recess. "What're we gonna talk about, our test marks? 'Ms. Bolton, you're full of it,' I might have to tell her. 'Ms. Bolton, this is great literature. Don't let punk spelling and punctuation turn you off. Don't think Shakespeare didn't have similar probs. Did he let that stop him? No siree.'

"I just might have to say that to her," Al said. "Then, when she's coming up for air, I hit her with the rabbit punch. I say, 'Ms. Bolton, ma'am, read between the lines. Ignore that other stuff. Taste the beautiful rhythm of the words. The symbolism. Memorable!' " Al closed her eyes and smacked her lips.

"Then I hit her again, when she's down. 'Ms. Bolton,' I say, 'if you don't change this mark to an A pronto, forget the freebie.' Whaddaya think?"

"That's blackmail," I said. "She might report us. Anyway, quit grousing. The whole thing was your idea in the first place. To ask her, I mean."

"You kidding me?" Al snorted. "I thought it was yours."

The day dragged. When the final bell rang, there

was a tremendous noisy exit. Kids deserted that room like rats leaving a sinking ship.

Simile? Aphorism? Whatever.

I noticed Martha Moseley stayed put. That meant she was waiting for everyone to clear out so she could nail Ms. Bolton and demand an explanation for her mark.

"We'll wait for you outside, Ms. Bolton," I said in a loud voice.

"In a minute," she said. Then I heard her say, "Martha, I can't talk right now. Could you come in early tomorrow? We'll go over your paper then."

As Al and I waited for Ms. Bolton, Al agonized, as was her wont.

"What if he forgets his freebie offer and hits us with a gigantic bill when it's over?" she said. "Suppose he turns nasty and bars the door until we cough up the cash? What then? He looks plenty skeevy to me. Sort of like a mobster."

"You wouldn't know a mobster if you fell over one," I told her.

"You know what I mean. He looks like a mobster in a movie." As she spoke, she paced back and forth at the top of the school steps. One false move and she'd hurtle to the bottom.

"Maybe we ought to call Teddy in for a mobster spot check," Al suggested. "He's the Mafia expert, after all. He'd give us the straight skinny. Is the guy a mobster or isn't he."

"Will you cut it out?" I said.

"Well, I sure hope nothing goes wrong," Al said. "If this whole health schmeer turns out to be a total bummer, then you just see what happens on your next paper. You think you lacked focus on this one, just wait until your next one. Man." Al hit herself on the forehead with such force she wobbled around for a while, looking spacey.

"Ms. Bolton's gonna hold it against us. Wait and see. See if I'm not right."

When she showed up, Ms. Bolton was smiling. She looked much younger than when she was in the classroom bawling, that's for sure. She also looked quite pretty.

"I'm really looking forward to this," she said. "When I woke up this morning, the first thing I thought was 'Today's workout day.' You would think at my age I could get myself to a gym on my own, but somehow I seem to have become immobilized since I moved here. Unhappiness does that to people, I guess. You get so mired in your own feelings it's tough to get out from under the rug."

She laughed and we did too.

We walked three abreast. The buildings stood out against the sky as if they'd been cut from construction paper. It was a windless day in mid-October and the temperature was just right.

"Is this guy who runs the health club a friend of yours?" Ms. Bolton asked us.

We told her about the pet shop turning into the health club practically overnight.

"His name's Al," I said. "Same as hers."

"Listen. My feeling about this guy is he's a total flake," Al said. "Don't expect too much, Ms. Bolton, O.K.?"

"I never do," she said.

A sign on the door of Al's Health Club said CLOSED.

"What'd I tell you." Al said. "It just opened. How can it be closed already?" We could see two men inside, talking. They didn't look like the same two we'd talked to.

"Knock," Al told me.

"Why don't you?" I said. She likes to give me orders, especially when we don't know what's what.

I knocked anyway. Somebody had to.

Nada. No response. Those bozos didn't give us the time of day. We went next door to the shoe-repair place and asked the man hammering away at somebody's new heels if he knew where Al was.

"I never seen him," the man said. I admired the way he talked with his mouth full of nails. He never swallowed one. "They come and they go over there. All day, all night. You can't tell nothing. Maybe you come back another day, huh?"

We were just about to give up when the door to Al's Health Club opened and the great man stood there, blinking in the light like he just got out of bed.

"Hi," Al and I said. "How are you?"

He drew a blank. It was plain he didn't remember us.

"You said we could have a free tryout," Al said. "Remember? You said word of mouth was the best advertising and we both have big mouths." She gave a nervous little laugh. I tried, but the best I could manage was a weak smile.

"You promised us a freebie," I said. My voice came out kind of squeaky. I cleared my throat. "You did. Really. We brought our teacher. She likes to work out too."

Al considered this information. Then he said, "Sure. You say so, I gotta believe you. Why not. I make you a promise, I keep it. Big Al's a man of his word. You better believe it. Come on in."

We followed him inside. It was kind of dark, and the two men at the back had disappeared.

"We got a problem with our electricity," Big Al told us. "Also with our deliveries. It's slow, starting up. Lot of headaches. But we'll make it. You want to change, there's a couple of rooms right there. You ladies slip into your sweats and I'll see to the equipment. I got a nice place here. I want it to run smooth, know what I mean?"

Al and I went into one of the changing rooms. Ms. Bolton went into the other.

"If he's Big Al," Al whispered, "then that makes me Little Al, right? Know something? I always wanted to be called Little Al. This is a first."

"Ouch," I said as her elbow got me in the eye. "Take it easy."

Al's underpants had SUNDAY written across them in bright red.

"It's Tuesday," I told her.

"*Now* you tell me," she said. "No wonder I don't know what day of the week it is. I'm always doing that."

My gym shorts were dirtier than I'd thought, but I pulled my baggy Mickey Mouse T-shirt down as far as it would go and it almost covered the shorts completely.

"You think we should go through with this?" I whispered to Al. She had on her gray sweat pants and sweatshirt. "I'm color coordinated," she said. "Sure, why not?"

We went out. Ms. Bolton was still in the changing room.

"O.K., girls," Big Al said. "This is your first workout?"

We nodded. Behind us, we heard Ms. Bolton's door open.

Big Al's eyes popped. He squeezed his nose with two fingers and closed his eyes. Then he opened them.

"Wooeee," Big Al sighed.

We turned. Ms. Bolton was dressed in a lime green leotard over a pink body suit.

She made Cher look out of shape.

Al and I were stunned, bowled over. To think that

she kept all her gorgeous self under wraps in her baggy clothes and her red tights.

Amazing.

"I've been working out since I was fifteen," Ms. Bolton said. "I used to be, well, not fat exactly, but sort of spongy. No muscle tone. My brothers turned me on to working out. They got me interested in lifting weights and running and doing sit-ups. Then I went to a fitness center and really got hooked. I can hardly wait to get back into doing that stuff. It makes me feel really great."

"Hey, miss, you wanna stand in my window for a couple hours?" Big Al said. "One look at you, they'll knock down the doors. How about it? I'd pay."

"I know," Al said. "Hang a sign on her that says AFTER and one on me that says BEFORE."

She gave Big Al a piercer.

"What's it worth?" she asked him.

"I'll hafta think about it," Big Al said.

Twelve

We walked up the fourteen flights of stairs to our floor when we got home, just in case Sparky's mom was hiding in the elevator, ready to pounce.

"Listen," Al said, breathing hard along about the tenth floor, "we better make up our minds about this darn party before I have a heart attack. I can't take all this exercise. First I do the rowing machine, then the jump rope, then the stationary bicycle. Now this. I'm basically a very weak person. I can't take life in the fast lane. So I'm out of shape. I guess I'm gonna stay that way."

"Well, let's call her and tell her we'll go, then," I

said. "It might be fun. And if we don't like her nephew, we just split and buzz for the elevator. It isn't as if we've got a long way to go."

Al dragged her key up out of her sweatshirt and unlocked her door. "Come on in," she said. "I've got something I want to show you."

"What?" I said.

Al was about to say more when her mother showed up, dangling one of Al's nerdy new shoes from the extreme tip of one finger. She was painfully distressed.

"Alexandra, what on earth happened?" Al's mother said. "How are you, dear?" she asked me. I used to be scared of her when Al first moved in down the hall, but now I like her.

"I smelled this perfectly foul odor," Al's mother continued, averting her eyes from the offending shoe, "and I traced it to your closet. Well, of course I immediately sprayed the whole place with Rume Fresh, but it still smells. What happened?"

Al gave her mother a shot of her bilious eyes.

"Sparky bombed me," she said.

"Who is Sparky? One of your friends?"

"Mom, Sparky is a dog," Al said. "He cornered me in the elevator and let fly on account of he took a dislike to me and my new shoes. And I hate 'em too. I wish you wouldn't buy me shoes, Mom. Let me buy my own, O.K.? Shoes are an expression of a person's personality and these don't express my personality, they express yours. I am an individual and these shoes offend me."

Then Al ran out of steam. She was like a balloon when the air goes out of it. She collapsed into the nearest chair.

"Why, Alexandra," her mother said, "I had no idea you felt that way. I thought they were rather chic."

"But I'm not chic, Mom," Al said, only she pronounced it "chick." "I'm a very down-to-earth person and I like down-to-earth shoes. I saw a pair of orange hightops to die over and I'm saving up for them. I don't want you to buy them for me. I want to buy them for myself."

Al's mother was a good sport. I saw her wince when Al said "orange hightops," but she recovered quickly.

"Our shoe department has a new spray they say brings back to life. I think I'll try it on these," and she waved Al's nerdy shoe around, keeping it safely away from her nose. "Would you girls like something to snack on? Carrot sticks or some celery?"

"How about a shot of tofu?" Al said. "Or a shooter of two percent milk."

"No, thanks," I said.

"O.K., come into my parlor so we can discuss something," Al said. "Begging your pardon, madam," she said to her mother, "but we need our privacy."

We zipped into her room and closed the door. Al

went to her desk and pulled out a scroungy little piece of paper.

"It's a letter I'm writing to Brian," she said.

"Oh, no, not again," I said. A while back, Al agonized a lot about a letter she was writing to Brian. Everybody got into the act. Tempers were short. She finally wound up signing it "Your Old Pal, Al" so he wouldn't think she was getting mushy.

"I might mail it, I might not," she said. "It depends."

"On what?" I said. "How about giving Mother Zandi a buzz, seeing what she advises."

"Good idea," Al said, and she dashed into her closet and emerged in her Mother Zandi turban, with the length of cloth Polly'd brought her from India wrapped around her sweat suit. Outside of looking kind of lumpy, she looked great. Very swami-ish.

After a suitable period, necessary to get her act together, Al peered into her imaginary crystal ball and said in her dark voice, "Mother Zandi says she who writes letter should mail said letter before postal rates rise. Better now than later, she says."

"Ask her about the party," I told Al.

Al was frowning into her crystal ball, charging her batteries, when Polly burst in.

"Your mother said you were in here," Polly said. "I decided to swing by when I got out of the dentist's and pin you guys down. Harry's biting his nails. Are you going or aren't you? I've built you up a lot and

Harry's psyched out for you to tea-dance with him. But he's getting nervous. I told him if you back out I'd ask Thelma. She's *dying* to go. Her mother told her never to say no to an invite on account of you never know who you might meet. Like, for instance, suppose the son of a king of a remote mountain principality in the Azores happens to be there and he asks you to visit him on his yacht next summer. Can you afford to pass that up?"

"You're telling us you'd throw a nice guy like Harry to the wolves?" Al asked indignantly. "Why, Thelma would eat Harry alive and ask for seconds."

"Well, Harry's got a brown belt in karate," Polly said. "I'm not too worried about him."

"First, we have to tell you what happened to us this afternoon," Al said. "It was truly bizarre."

I have to admit we embellished it some, but basically we told the whole truth. Polly was entranced. "Go on, what happened next?" she kept saying.

It *was* a pretty good story. Not your basic, run-of-the-mill after-school special. Besides, Polly was a very satisfying person to tell a story to. She reacted so wonderfully.

"I don't believe it!" Polly shrieked when we described how Ms. Bolton had emerged from the changing room and how Big Al's mouth had dropped open at the sight of her gorgeous bod. How he'd said if she posed in his window he'd pay her, that they'd take one look at her and break down the doors.

"How about if I go with you next time you go there?" Polly suggested. "I could use a little of that body-building routine."

"If there *is* a next time," Al said. "We've run out of freebies and he'd probably want us to sign up for six months or something like that."

"How come you're dressed up like that, Al?" Polly said. "It isn't time to get suited up for Halloween yet, is it?"

"She's Mother Zandi," I explained. "Al's got another letter in the works to Brian, and Mother Zandi's giving her advice."

"Yiyiyiyiyi," Polly crooned, closing her eyes and swaying back and forth. "Another letter to old Brian, eh? I can't handle it, kids. I'm off. What's the word for me to carry to Harry? This is your last chance."

"Tell you what," Al said. "I'll get Mother Zandi on the line, and after I check about the party for Sparky's mom's brilliant nephew, I'll get the vibes on Harry's thé dansant."

Al rearranged her turban and leaned heavily into her crystal ball, and Polly said, "Sparky? Sparky's mom's nephew? What is this, anyway? I hope it's not contagious. You guys must be on something. I'm leaving before I catch what you've got. Who's Sparky?"

Al and I exchanged a long, significant look.

"Should we?" Al asked me. "Tell her, I mean."

I thought about it.

"O.K.," I finally said. "But maybe you should leave out the really good parts. She's only a kid."

So we told her. And the way we told the story, it took quite a long time.

Thirteen

The next morning was chaotic.

My mother had one of her migraines.

My father was tight-lipped, the way he gets when she has one of her headaches. They immobilize her. She stays in bed with the shades pulled for two or three days until the migraine goes away.

I hate it when my mother's sick. The whole house goes topsy turvy.

"Maybe I should stay home," I started to say. But my father thought he heard her calling and dashed away. Teddy opened his mouth, which was full of half-eaten breakfast, and pushed his face close to mine. My stomach lurched.

"Listen, cretin." I took Teddy by the scruff of his neck and talked fast and low. "One false move and you're dead meat. It's out the window with you. And I don't think I have to remind you we're fourteen floors up, right?"

I heard my father coming back and let go of Teddy.

"She'd like a cup of tea," my father told me.

"I'll fix it," I said. "You want me to stay home, Dad?"

"That won't be necessary. Rest is what she needs. But you'd better come straight home from school to see if you can do anything for her. She may want something to eat by then. I've got an early meeting." He checked his watch. "I better get going. When your mother is laid low, I expect both of you to behave. No bickering, no horsing around. Think of her, not of yourselves, please. Teddy, are you listening?"

Teddy took his finger out of his nose and stuffed it into his ear. He kind of nodded and didn't make a peep.

Stiffly my father bent to kiss both of us.

I fixed the tea and thought about how Al stood by her mother last summer. How she gave up going to the barn dance and everything. She never complained. Never once.

The fact is, I didn't want to stay home. Al and I had plans to swing by the health club after school to see what was up. We liked that place. It was full of odd-balls, weirdos we found fascinating. A couple of blondes came in yesterday as we were leaving. They were pretty tough kahunas with big muscles and lots of makeup. I wished they'd come earlier. I would've loved to see them in action, but Al kept pulling on my arm, saying "Don't wear out your welcome, kid."

I carried the tray to my mother's room.

"Mom," I whispered. My mother lay with one arm over her eyes. "You want anything?"

"I'll be fine." Her voice sounded thin. "Just promise me you'll be nice to Teddy. Try not to fight. Try to be friends. Please."

I promised. Luckily Teddy and my father were gone when I went back to the kitchen. I brushed my teeth and got my books, and when I went into the hall Al was standing by the elevator, waiting for me.

"Teddy said your mother was sick," she said. "I'm sorry."

"Sure," I said. I didn't feel like talking.

The elevator lurched to a stop at our floor. Inside, smiling at us, were Sparky and his mom. Well, *she* was smiling, he wasn't.

"Wonderful! I couldn't have planned it better!" Sparky's mom cried. "I just knew I'd catch you sooner or later!"

The sound of her voice gave me a headache. I wasn't up for polite conversation. We rode in silence. I heard Sparky grunting at me but pretended he wasn't there. One false move from Sparky, I decided, and he'd be dead meat, just like Teddy.

"Sixish on Saturday, girls!" Sparky's mom cried as we crash-landed in the lobby. "Just wear anything!" and she and the mutt sailed out into the street.

"She doesn't know it," Al muttered, "but that's what I was planning on wearing. We didn't say we'd go to her party, did we?"

"I didn't," I said. "I don't know about you."

"Well, she expects us. We don't want to hurt her feelings," Al said.

"She'd never notice if we did," I said.

Usually Al walks fast and I trail behind. Today, I was in the lead and she was behind.

"I feel like a million bucks," Al said. "I sweated like a pig yesterday. I guess that's why."

"Pigs don't sweat," I said.

"Actually, man is the only animal that sweats," Al said. "That's why deodorants were invented."

"I have to go straight home after school," I said. "My mother has one of her migraines. I promised my father I would."

"That's O.K. We can swing by the health club tomorrow," Al said. "No sweat."

"You sure have sweat on the brain today," I said.

Al looked at me but didn't say anything. I guess I could be in the pits as much as she could if I felt like it.

When we went into our homeroom Ms. Bolton was at her desk wearing her usual baggy duds. Plus her red tights. I felt as if I'd imagined yesterday.

But no. "Thanks a million for yesterday," she said to Al and me. "It was wonderful. I can't tell you how much it raised my spirits to work out again. I'm trying to figure out how I can afford to sign up at the health club for six months. Maybe if I give up eating, I can swing it." She laughed and, although it was an effort, so did I.

After last bell rang, I got my stuff together.

"You go without me," I told Al. "Say hello to Big Al for me."

She shook her head. "I'm going home, too," she said. "Maybe I can sit with your mother in case you have to go to the store or anything. Maybe I could read to her or something. Maybe she'd like me to read the paper to her if she doesn't know what went on today."

"Chances are not only does she not know, but doesn't give a darn," I said. But I was glad Al was coming with me instead of going to Big Al's.

We let ourselves into my apartment. I put my books on the hall table and said, "I'll just go and see . . ."

A man came out of the living room.

We both jumped.

It was my grandfather. He said, "Hello, darling," to me. Then he saw Al and said, "How's my gal Al?"

My grandfather often calls me darling. But when he said that to Al, she turned beet red with pleasure. Al doesn't have a grandfather. She thinks mine is the best. For her birthday he gave her a book by Ring

Lardner called *I Know You, Al.* This book was very famous in its day. Al loves it.

"What are you doing here?" I asked my grandfather.

"Looking after your mother," he said. "Your father called me to let me know she was under the weather. I thought I might be of some help. She's asleep now. I look in on her now and then. Now that you're home, I'll take myself off."

My grandfather is extremely handsome. He's a young sixty-six. That's an oxymoron, which means a contradiction in terms. I looked it up. How can anyone sixty-six be young? It's possible. He asked Al's mother out on a date a while back. Al told me that if they got married she and I would be related. Give her the ball and she really runs with it. One date and she's got them tying the knot.

She's too much.

My grandfather put his hat on. He always wears a hat, even in summer.

"Your mother's asleep now," he said. "I just looked in on her. If you need me, call."

"Thanks a million," I said. "It was very nice of you to come."

"She'd do the same for me," my grandfather said. He kissed me and he and Al shook hands.

When he'd gone, Al said, "Know who he reminds me of?"

"Cary Grant," I said.

"No." Al shook her head. "Mr. Richards."

"Mr. Richards! You're cuckoo," I told her. "Mr. Richards had blue eyes and my grandfather's are brown. Plus Mr. Richards didn't have a cleft in his chin."

"So what? None of that matters. Your grandfather's a class act," Al said, very serious, "and Mr. Richards is a class act."

"Was" I almost said, then let it alone.

The more I thought about it, the more I knew she was right. Mr. Richards and my grandfather *were* alike. It was a new and strangely comforting thought.

Fourteen

That night I made eggplant parmigiana for dinner. Teddy hates eggplant parmigiana in the worst way. That's not my fault. I found a withered eggplant in the fridge and a bottle of spaghetti sauce in the cupboard. Polly would have a fit. She thinks bottled spaghetti sauce is the pits. Anyway, I put them together with plenty of cheese and it wasn't bad. My father ate hastily without really knowing what he ate. Teddy made a small gagging sound and I nailed him with a super-duper piercer, so he shut up and pushed the eggplant around on his plate.

It's funny about eggplant; they tell you to salt the

slices then let them sit for half an hour. The eggplant sweats. You have to rinse it off. I bet Al doesn't know that eggplant sweats. She thinks she knows practically everything, but there are a couple of things she's missed.

My father excused himself to go sit with my mother. He took her some tea and toast.

"I'll do the dishes and you sweep the floor," I told Teddy.

He took the broom and started waving it around like it was a sword.

Al rang her ring.

"I'll get it," I said. Teddy hit me on the head with his broom and I swatted him on the behind with the dishcloth.

"I said I'd get it," I told Teddy, brandishing the rolling pin, which I'd snatched from the drawer. "Don't forget Mom's sick and Dad's home. Just keep your nose clean, buddy, and all will be well."

"I hope I didn't wake your mother if she was sleeping," Al whispered. "I rang the bell as quietly as I could."

"Come on in," I said. "It's O.K. My father's with her. What's that on your head?"

She beamed. "Isn't it strappy?" she said. "I made it. It's a sweat band."

Her bangs stuck straight out like a porcupine's quills.

"I think you've got it on wrong," I said. "Your hair

looks funny. Why don't you stick your bangs under instead of over?"

"This is the way you're supposed to wear a sweat band," Al said.

"I've got KP duty tonight," I said. "Come on out. You can help me clean up." Teddy had disappeared. With any luck, maybe he'd locked himself into the refrigerator. Either that or he was in the broom closet sniffing glue.

"How'd you make it?" I asked Al because I knew she wanted me to ask.

"I read it in a magazine. I cut off the bottom of my old sweatshirt," she said, "and then I sewed on buttons and glitz and stuff around it. Whadya think, is it gorge or is it gorge?"

"You look sort of like a porcupine," I told her. "With your bangs sticking out like that."

"How do you know what a porcupine looks like?" she said in a cross voice.

"I saw a TV special about porcupines. They have these quills, and when a dog or some kind of animal attacks them they fire the quills and boy, do they hurt. You have to take the dog to the vet and he puts the dog out and pulls the quills out one by one."

"I think it's pretty cool," Al said. Meaning her sweat band.

"What did your mother say when she saw it?" I asked her.

"What she always says: 'It doesn't do anything

for you, Alexandra,' Al said in an imitation of her mother's voice. "What she refuses to recognize is that *nothing* does anything for me. How's your mother feeling?"

"About the same. It usually takes two or three days for her to feel like herself. She should be fine by Saturday."

"You know, when my mother was in the hospital," Al said, turning somber, "I planned what I'd do if she didn't come out."

"Come out? You mean if she died?" I said, astonished. There had never been any suggestion that Al's mother would *die*. At least, not that I know of.

"Yes. If she died." Al pronounced each word with great care. "I don't have that many relatives, you know. Of course, there's my father. He's a relative."

"Yeah, that's true," I said. "A father's a relative, all right."

"But don't forget he has another family now," Al said. "And even though they like me and we're all friends, that doesn't mean they want me living with them. Visiting is one thing, living is another. Everybody needs his space, right?" Al peered out at me from under her sweat band and she looked so mournful I almost laughed. But I've learned not to laugh at Al when she's mournful, so I just nodded and kept quiet.

"When you live with people, all sorts of little irritating things happen," Al went on. "Like you leave the top off the toothpaste, for instance. Or you hum while you're eating. Or you talk with your mouth full. You get on people's nerves without even knowing you're doing it. That can spoil a beautiful friendship. So I'm not sure I should go live with my father and Louise and the boys if anything happens to my mother. She's used to me, after all."

"Hey, give your mother a break," I said. "She's doing fine. You said so yourself. She looks great." I wondered why we were having this conversation.

"So I planned what I'd do." Al went on as if I hadn't spoken. "If my mother died, that is."

"O.K.," I said. "Spit it out."

"I thought I'd join a cloistered order of nuns," she told me, her eyes huge.

"But you're not even Catholic," I said.

"You don't have to be born Catholic," she said. "You can convert."

"What do cloistered nuns do?" I said.

"They take a vow of silence," Al said. "They spend—"

"A vow of silence!" I said. "You'd flip if you took a vow of silence. You'd absolutely, positively go out of your brains. And you know it."

"Oh, I don't know," Al said, in a huff. "Just because you couldn't take a vow of silence doesn't mean *I* couldn't handle it. I'd probably make a pretty good cloistered nun."

"Yeah, I can see you now," I said. "You've got this thing you have to tell me. I mean, it's burning a hole in your mouth if you can't spit it out, if you can't zip down the hall and lay it all out. Yeah, some cloistered nun you'd make," and I burst out laughing.

"That's all you know," Al said, still in a huff. Then the corners of her mouth began to twitch and lift, and before she knew it she was rolling on the floor, clutching her stomach, laughing so hard she couldn't stop.

When we'd calmed down, Al said, "Do you think a mother should die before her children do?"

"Holy Toledo," I said. "I don't know. I never thought of it." Which wasn't strictly true. I have thought of it. There was a girl in my class whose mother died last year. It was the saddest thing I ever saw. Her face was without any joy, any fun, and before, she'd been very lively and full of mischief.

My mother says she wants to die before we do, Teddy and I. She says she's not sure about dying before my father does, but she definitely will not put up with us dying before she does. She jokes when she says this, but I can tell she means it. "But if I die before your father does," my mother says, fooling around, "I want you to make sure no designing female gets her mitts on him. If, after a suitable span of time, you can find him a nice, kind woman who's a good cook and fond of you children, well, all right. But keep your eyes out for conniving women. There are lots of them around."

"How did we get on this subject, anyway?" I said. "Your mother's in great shape and so's mine."

"It doesn't do any harm to think things through and make plans," Al said. "If I didn't become a cloistered nun, I might go to work in an old-people's home, like the one Mr. Keogh's father's in."

"Yeah, then you could tell fortunes and be Mother Zandi," I said.

"My mother's going to a gala affair on Saturday," Al said.

"So are we," I said.

"We are?"

"Yeah. At Sparky's mom's place," I said. "I'm going along as your chaperone in case the nephew gets rowdy."

Al did a few bumps and grinds. "You think that's a possibility?" she said.

Fifteen

Friday was a school holiday, because there was a teacher's convention. My mother was feeling much better. She thanked me for taking care of her and being such a big help. She thanked Teddy too, but I figure she sort of had to.

"I'm proud of you," she said. "You really took over and ran the house."

"Yeah," Teddy said. "We sure did."

"Why don't you and Al do something fun today? You deserve a break." She gave me five dollars and said, "Don't spend it all in one place."

"Let's go check the mink coats at F A O Schwarz," I said.

Ever since Al's mother brought home an F A O Schwarz catalogue that advertised, among other exotic playthings, mink coats in sizes 2T, 4T, and 6T, we'd planned on going down to inspect the joint. F A O Schwarz has got to be the most fantastic toy store in the world.

T stands for toddler, I told Al.

"Surreal," Al said.

"Let's go," I said.

We took the bus. It was raining.

The driver was an old crank. Sometimes the drivers were really nice. They sing and make little jokes and are kind to old ladies who don't walk very well. This one slammed the brakes on and snarled at anyone who asked him for a transfer or whether this bus stopped at Forty-second Street.

We sat in the back, right over a heater that was sending forth blasts of hot air.

"Get the picture," Al said, waving her hands to send the heat my way. "This four-year-old kid who is spoiled rotten, due to the fact both parents are lawyers and making big bucks so they believe in quality time instead of quantity time and give the kid anything she wants, gets a mink coat for her birthday. It's a 6T on account of even rich folks like their kids to get two seasons out of their outerwear. So the kid goes to the park with her nanny in her mink coat. All kids wearing mink coats have to have a nanny. That's a rule. The kid's also got a power bike with a V-8 engine, which she plans to enter in the Grand Prix when she grows up.

"And in the park lurks this nefarious guy who keeps tabs on kids wearing genuine mink. He hangs out there and chats up the nannies while they're sitting tatting on the park bench, demure as heck, hoping some bigwig TV producer will discover them and put them in a sit com."

"Tatting?" I said.

"Yeah. It's like knitting only it's tatting," Al said. "So the guy chats up the nanny, tells her he's a retired bank president or something soothing like that. He says isn't her charge a little doll, stuff like that. He even carries a bag full of sour balls that he hands out. Then, while he's got the nanny's attention, his cohort sneaks up on the kid, who's riding her power bike in her mink coat and really working up a sweat.

"Talk about sweat!" Al rolled her eyes and her eyebrows went flying up underneath her bangs. "Try riding a power bike while you're wearing a mink coat. Man, it's the most! Anyway, the cohort walks right in front of the kid's bike so the kid brakes, and the cohort, who is very swift, rips the fur coat off the kid before she even gets her thumb out of her mouth. By the time she catches on and starts hollering, the cohort's over the river and through the woods with the goods."

Al took a breather. Story telling is very draining work, she says.

"So what does the cohort do with the size 6T mink?" I asked her.

"Well, he hands it over to his own kid, who's only two but fast growing. But when the kid's wicked stepmother gets a load of the coat, she goes ape. She says if he doesn't get her a mink coat in her size, she'll rat to the fuzz. The End."

"No," I said. "That's not what happens. This is what happens."

Al watched me closely. She's very jealous about her stories. She wants them to go her way. Before I knew Al, I never made up stories. Now I'm getting pretty good at it.

I cleared my throat.

"The guy who rips off the kid's coat owns a doggy boutique," I said. "They sell doggy silk pajamas and bikinis and plaid bathrobes for lounging in. The guy cuts up the kid's mink coat and makes it into little muffs and belly bands for tiny dogs about Sparky's size. Dog lovers go beserk. Sparky's mom buys him a complete outfit. Sparky and his mom go on TV talk shows, the whole bit. They're instant celebrities."

I looked at Al. She pretended to be dozing.

"Pretty good, huh?" I said.

"What's a belly band?" Al asked, with her eyes still closed.

"It's what they used to put around a newborn baby's belly to make sure the belly button didn't fall off and get lost," I said.

"I never heard of such a thing," Al said.

"Just because you never heard of it," I said, "doesn't mean it doesn't exist."

The bus slowed for our stop.

"Maybe the toddler furs are on sale today," Al said. "Let us hasten inside and see what's up."

"Which way are the toddler fur coats?" we asked the man who paces back and forth in front of the store and opens taxi doors for customers.

He pointed upward. I think he was giving us the finger, but Al said, "Thank you, sir," to put him in his place.

First thing we saw was a Ferrari in kid's size that actually runs.

"How much?" we asked the man standing guard.

"Fifteen K," he said.

"What's K mean?" Al said.

"Thousand," the man said.

"Charge it," we said, and zipped up on the escalator.

We checked out the gold-plated carousel and a nine-foot-tall stuffed giraffe. We ogled the black-walnut rocking horse and the miniature baby grand piano. But we never did find the toddler minks.

When we'd had our fill, we went back down and out.

"Unreal," I said.

"Pure sci fi," Al agreed.

"Let's go check the Russian Tea Room," I suggested.

The Russian Tea Room is close to F A O Schwarz. It's a celebrity hangout where the celebs chow down on caviar and blinis.

"There's Woody Allen!" I hissed.

"Where?"

"There. Just going into the Russian Tea Room. Don't speak to him, though. He gets very upset when fans say 'Hi, Woody Loved your last picture.' He likes to travel incognito. That's why he always skulks around with his collar pulled way up."

"Why doesn't he just eat lunch at home, then?" Al said.

"Polly said she saw Donald Trump coming out once," I said.

"Phooey on Donald Trump," Al said. "Let's shoot for a biggy like Jackie Onassis or Andy Rooney."

"How about Shirley Temple?" I said. "I read she was autographing copies of her autobiography this week. I wouldn't mind seeing her. She's about our age, you know. I bet we'd have lots in common."

"You're crazy," Al said. "She's old. She's a grandmother and everything."

"I saw her on the silver screen only last week," I said. "She looked pretty young to me."

"I understand she wears a wig," Al said.

We hung around, but Woody didn't show. Neither did any other celebrity.

"You want to go to Carnegie Hall?" I said.

"How do you get to Carnegie Hall?" Al said. Then,

before I could beat her to it, she said, "Practice, baby, practice."

"That's as old as the hills," I said. "I heard my grandfather say that years ago."

"If we had any moola," Al said, "we could take a hansom cab through the park."

"People always stare at people in hansom cabs," I said. "I'd hate having all those people staring at me, thinking I was a rich tourist or something."

"Maybe the Rockefeller Plaza skating rink is open," Al said. "We could go down and watch them twirl."

"Too early," I said. "Anyway, I hate to skate there. I fall down too much and everybody stares. It's embarrassing."

"Hey, you're getting a real complex about people staring at you, kid," Al told me.

"Yeah, I know."

"All right, sports fans, let's try Radio City Music Hall, see if we can get in for the Christmas show," Al said.

"It hasn't started yet, dummy," I said.

"We might have to give up and go home," Al said.

"Let's walk," I said. It had stopped raining.

We walked east, across to Park Avenue. Park Avenue's fun to walk up, it's so sort of snazzy.

"I read that when Shirley Temple was fourteen the Hollywood moguls wanted to keep her a child star as long as they could, so they bound her bust," Al told me.

"No kidding?" I said. "That's a good idea. Why don't we try that?"

"I thought we already had," Al said.

We laughed until we both came down with the hiccups.

"Hey, look!" I grabbed Al's arm. "I don't believe it. Twice in one day. It's Woody again."

Al squinted into the distance.

"You may be right," she said. "Let's say hello."

"Hi, Woody," we said. "Loved your last picture."

The little man in the big glasses looked startled, then alarmed. Then he pulled up his collar even further and scuttled off, incognito.

Sixteen

Saturday my father and I tossed a coin. He got to do the vacuuming and the marketing and I wound up with the bathrooms. This is not uncommon when we flip a coin. Sometimes I wonder about that coin, about whether it's on the level.

Teddy was the designated duster.

My grandfather called and said he'd like to take us out to dinner.

My mother said she'd love to but how about next week.

My mother's sister, Tess, called from Connecticut. When she found out my mother had been sick, she offered to come and stay to help out.

"I'll send the kids to their father," Tess said. "Serve him right."

"How's things up in Mafia land?" Teddy hollered over the wire to Craig, the know-it-all cousin. When Teddy talks to Connecticut, he acts as if he's got a bad connection to Istanbul.

"Had any good drug busts lately?" Teddy shouted across the miles. I didn't hear what Craig reported.

Al came over and I made cream-cheese-and-olive sandwiches. On whole-wheat bread. It's important to use whole-wheat bread.

"My mother said to tell your mother that if there was anything she could do, let her know," Al said.

"Know something?" I said. "We've got the perfect excuse. We call up Sparky's mom and tell her we can't come tonight on account of we have to stay home and take care of my mother."

"Saturday night is the loneliest night in the week," Al said. "It's also blind-date night. If I don't do it now, I never will. It's a challenge. It's practice. I've got my outfit all planned. I'm playing it straight. This nephew strikes me as a straight guy. I'm wearing my lavender sweater, my plaid skirt, and on my feet—guess!" She let fly with a piercer.

"Your orange hightops?" I guessed.

"My Sparky's-revenge shoes," she said. She said she wanted to see whether Sparky remembered those shoes, and that if he did and he repeated his barf-pee routine, she was planning on poisoning him and burying him in an unmarked grave.

"I'm planning on wearing my taffeta party dress," I said.

Slowly, Al shook her head at me. "That's being over-dressed," she told me. "We do not want to go to this fracas overdressed, thereby revealing that we expect great things of it. We want to be underdressed. My mother, who is in fashion, as you know, says it's always better to underdress than over."

We thrashed through my limited wardrobe awhile.

"My taffeta dress is the only garment I have that *does* anything for me," I said.

"Forget the taffeta dress," Al commanded me. "It's the light of intelligence shining from your eyes that'll get him in the long run. Nothing else matters." At last, we settled on my denim skirt and my Esprit shirt, which my mother bought from a street vendor on Sixth Avenue. It's phony Esprit, but it's sort of cute. In a trendy way.

"Where are you two bound for?" my father asked from behind his newspaper.

"We're going to meet Sparky's mom's nephew," I told him. He didn't turn a hair.

"It's a blind date," I added, testing him.

He put his paper down. "A blind date? Are you old enough for a blind date? I thought they were out of style. I remember a blind date I had when I was in college."

Al and I looked at each other. My father? On a blind date? In college?

"I was a very young freshman," he said. "Very naive. Still wet behind the ears, as my father used to say. My roommate had a date with a girl he knew from home and he fixed me up with a friend of his date's. I even got a haircut in anticipation. He said she was a hot number."

My father looked at us.

"That's the way young men referred to women in those days," he said. "I apologize for any sexism you can find in that statement."

My father really does track at times, I was glad to discover. That's one of the things that makes him so lovable. Just when you think he's out of it, he jumps back in.

"Anyway," he continued, "we drove to the meeting place and I was so nervous I told my roommate I couldn't go through with it. He said it was too late to turn back now. He was right. The girls were waiting. They were sitting down. I remember thinking my date had terrific legs. She was also the better looking of the two. To my eyes, she was very glamorous, very sophisticated.

"Well, when she stood up, she towered over me. Of course, she wore high heels, but even flat footed she towered over me. We were supposed to go to a dance. My date was all dressed up in something frilly. She was a very kind girl, though. Because, without any commotion, she let me know it was fine with her if we stayed put. Or maybe she couldn't face dancing with me at all. Whatever the reason, it turned out all right. We parted friends."

"I never saw her again," my father said, a little wistfully, I thought.

"That was a very romantic story," Al said afterward.

"I thought it was sad," I said. "I felt bad for him."

"Your father is a very romantic man," Al told me.

"You think so?"

"Extremely so," Al said firmly.

I made a mental note to ask my mother about this.

"What time is it?" I asked Al.

"Well, last time I looked, it was six-oh-one," Al said. She checked her Swatch and said, "It is now six-oh-four."

"We don't want to look eager and get there too early," I said.

"We can always eat and run," Al said. "I'm starving. No offense, but that cream cheese and olive wasn't all that filling."

"I would've made you another if you'd asked," I said. "Let's go."

"Wait just one sec," Al said, and she made one more trip to the bathroom.

"Blind dates are very nerve-wracking," she told me on her return.

At six-oh-twelve we rang Sparky's mom's bell.

We laid our ears against the door, listening. There was lots of noise coming from inside.

"It's probably an orgy," Al told me, smoothing her hair.

"Yes?" The person who at last answered the door had eyes like two poached eggs, and when he talked I noticed his Adam's apple bobbed like kids going for apples on Halloween.

Al positioned herself behind me, ready to bolt if this guy turned out to be her blind date. I felt her tugging nervously on my skirt, telling me it was time to split.

What the heck. We'd been invited, hadn't we?

"Hi," I said.

"Whom shall I say is calling?" the person with the Adam's apple asked.

"Are you the butler?" I asked.

Al turned to me and said, "Whom are we, anyway?"

"We're the girls from the elevator," I said.

Sparky's mom swept into view, as if she'd been hiding behind the door.

"Oh, there you are!" she cried, happy to see us. "I thought you'd never get here." She had on a skin-tight black jumpsuit and a huge gold necklace that came halfway down her chest and clanked noisily.

"Come meet Josh. He's dying to meet you. I've told him all about you two." She took me by the hand and dragged me into the fray. I grabbed Al's hand and brought her along with me. If she thought she was going to escape at this stage of the game, she had another think coming.

My mother told me to check out the decor. She likes to know about colors of slipcovers, walls, rugs, et cetera. The room was so crowded it was hard to see much. I noticed an old woman with white skin and bright red hair, holding an unlit cigarette in a long holder and waving her long-nailed hands around. Others moved in what seemed like slow motion, laughing, talking, drinking, flicking ashes into the potted palms.

"Josh, darling! Did I promise you some lovely girls?" Sparky's mom sounded positively joyous. "Don't say I never do anything for you. Here they are."

"Ta dah," I heard Al whisper.

Josh reclined in a big chair, his legs draped over the arm. The first thing I noticed was his high-heeled cowboy boots. They were dark red, the color of old blood, and beautiful. He wore chinos and a button-down shirt. He didn't get up, only lifted a hand in greeting.

"Hey," he said. "Have a seat."

"I'm thirsty," Al said.

"Of course you're thirsty," Sparky's mom said, as if we'd traveled mile after dusty mile to reach this place. "Come with me and I'll show you where the refreshments are. Don't go away, darling," she said to Josh, who looked as if he might fall asleep.

"He's so shy," Sparky's mom said as we plunged through the crowd. "Be nice to him, will you? He needs attention, friends, love."

"Who doesn't?" Al muttered under her breath.

"Just help yourselves," Sparky's mom said. Then she turned to speak to someone and drifted out of sight.

"How tall is he?" Al asked me.

"In or out of his boots?" I said. "Have a shooter of Coke. You need sweetening."

Al and I picked. We ate stuffed mushrooms, nachos, and crudités, which is French for carrot sticks.

"Maybe we better go back and talk to him," I said after a while.

"Heck with that," Al said. "Let him come and talk to us. Listen," she said, frowning, "I have a hunch the guy might be a midget. I knew I should've checked out how tall he was before I got suckered into this mess."

"Don't be such a pill," I told her. "It's a party. Smile. Act as if you're enjoying yourself."

When we got back to where Josh had been, he was gone.

"Maybe someone kidnapped him," Al said, noticeably brightening.

"You wish," I said.

"Hey." The call came from a nearby couch.

"Rats," Al said.

Josh had a friend with him. He had big chipmunk

cheeks and aviator glasses and wore a vest.

"He must be your date," Al said, grinning for the first time.

We didn't know where else to go, so we walked over.

"This is Mark," Josh performed the introductions. "He's my best buddy."

The four of us chatted up a storm.

"So what's new in the Big Apple?" Mark said.

"Where are you guys from?" Al asked.

"Cincinnati," Mark said.

"What do you do for kicks in Cincinnati?" Al said.

"We mostly hang out at the mall," Mark said. Josh may have fallen asleep by then, for all we knew. He sure wasn't talking.

"Lots of action going on at the mall." Mark smiled slyly.

"Give me a for instance," Al said.

"Oh," Mark said, surprised. "The usual. You know. Dates, dances, flicks, video games."

"Oh, wow," Al said.

I said, "We don't have malls in the city," because I thought it was time for me to say something.

"Well, what do *you* do for kicks?" Josh asked. "Go for walks in Central Park and wait to be mugged?"

"We're into health clubs, weight lifting, Nautilus machines, all that," Al said nonchalantly. "Sometimes we take in a jazz joint or two, if it starts getting really late. I mean, those joints don't get a buzz on until well after midnight."

"Jazz, huh." Josh whipped out a pocket knife and started to clean his fingernails. "I'm into Willie Nelson. Willie's my boy."

"How come no socks?" Al asked, pointing to Mark's bare ankles.

Mark clutched himself, as if to warm the ankles, and said, "We don't wear socks in Cincinnati. It's not cool."

"Whaddaya do when it snows?" Al said.

Josh put his hand over his mouth and whispered something in Mark's ear.

"My mother always told me it was impolite to whisper," I said. I know I sounded like an awful prig, but she did say that and I believe it's true.

Suddenly Josh said, "Like your shoes," to Al. "They're very, very funky."

"You do?" Al's eyes widened in surprise. "They're yours." And she started to remove her shoes. Both boys backed off.

"We got something to tell you," Josh said. He jabbed Mark in the ribs. "Tell 'em, boy," he ordered.

"Josh wants me to tell you he has the major hots for Diane," Mark said solemnly.

"No kidding?" Al said in her supersarcastic voice.

"Just in case you get any ideas," Josh said. "Diane has a body that won't quit."

Al and I traded looks.

"Well, Al wants me to tell you she has the major hots for Brian and he has muscles that won't quit," I said. "He also works out and he's very, very jealous."

Al put her shoes back on and said, "We better split. Nice knowing you."

The boys from Cincinnati zoned out. I guess they figured they were in way over their heads with us city girls. We looked for Sparky's mom to say thank you for a nice time, but she wasn't around.

"Talk about wet behind the ears!" Al exploded when we hit the elevator button to take us down to home and safety.

"What's with the shoe bit?" I said.

"Well, you know how you read about some rich eccentric person, how when someone says 'I like your diamond ring' or 'I like your gold watch' the rich eccentric person whips off the watch or the ring and says, 'It's yours,' and hands it over to the person who admired it. I've always wanted to do that. It's a beau geste." Al gave me her owl eye. "So I figure if the bozo from Cincinnati admires my funky shoes, they're his. I unload 'em on just the right person. The thing of it is"—and Al turned melancholy—"they would've been way too big. His feet were eensy."

She sucked her cheeks in and crossed her eyes.

"Social encounters of the third kind are extremely taxing," she said. "I'm whipped."

"What time is it?" I said.

"Seven-oh-seven," Al said, checking her Swatch. "Come on in and I'll nuke us a couple of hot dogs and we can play Russian Bank. You don't want to go home this early. Your mother and father will think you didn't have a good time."

"I like your watch," I said as Al opened the door.

She turned and looked at me over her shoulder.

"Tough beans, baby," she said.

Seventeen

"How'd it go?" my father asked. "Meet any cute boys?"

"Well, not exactly cute," I said. "Kind of weird, actually."

"Oh? Where from?" he said.

"Cincinnati," I said.

"Oh, Cincinnati," my father said.

"Let's put it this way, Dad," I told him. "It wasn't exactly love at first sight."

"It almost never is," he said.

When I brought my mother breakfast in bed on Sunday morning, I told her Al and I planned to go to the health club that afternoon.

"Health club?" she said. "I don't think a health club's exactly the kind of place a girl of your age should go. Isn't it full of seedy, sweaty people?"

"Mom, we're not talking pool hall here," I said. "We're talking fitness. It's where people go to work out and firm up their bodies. Mostly the people are yuppie types. Power brokers, that kind of stuff. They lift weights and all that."

"Yeah, and they all look like Cher, I bet," she said. "In my day, weight lifters were not considered suitable companions for thirteen-year-old girls," and she shot me a piercer over the rim of her orange-juice glass.

"Mom, things are different now," I said.

"Oh, don't give me that," she said.

"These guys just opened the business," I said, "and they're looking for customers. Our teacher, Ms. Bolton, went there and it turned out she's really into working out. She's got a figure that won't quit, although you'd never know it on account of she wears clothes that are very big for her."

"What's *that* mean, a figure that won't quit?" my mother asked.

"I don't know," I admitted. "This guy we met at the party yesterday said his girlfriend had a figure that won't quit, so I told him Al had a boyfriend named Brian with muscles that won't quit. I figured that ought to fix him."

"And did it?" my mother said, trying not to laugh.

"Who knows. They were nerdy types from Cincinnati."

"Oh, Cincinnati," my mother said. "I used to go out with a boy from Cincinnati. I was crazy about him. Then I noticed he kept track of every penny he spent, wrote the dollars and cents down in a little book he carried with him. I decided maybe he wasn't good husband material. It's the little things that count, don't forget."

"I'll clean up the kitchen," I said. She hadn't said I couldn't go.

"Be home by five," my mother told me. "You know I worry if you're out after dark."

I almost said, "It doesn't get dark until six" but decided against it. No sense in pushing my luck.

"I'm glad you're better, Mom," I said. "Al said when her mother went to the hospital she planned on who she'd live with if her mother died. She said I didn't have to worry if anything happened to you because I have more family than she does."

"It seems to me you and Al are awfully ready to wipe us off the face of the map if we spend a couple of days in bed," my mother said, fluffing up her back hair the way Thelma does, but quietly, on account of she doesn't wear bangle bracelets.

I kissed her. "You're a good woman, Mom," I told her.

"Go on and go," she said. "And comb your hair. It's a mess."

Al and I ate standing up so we wouldn't dirty the clean counters. "I like your hair that way," I told her. Her mother had fixed Al's hair in a French braid.

"Yeah. She said it makes my face look thinner. Between you and me, I think she's full of it," Al said glumly. "I'm up for cheek surgery. How about it?" She blew out her cheeks at me.

"You look like a blowfish," I said.

"I am making a fashion statement," Al said. "One minute I'm in pigtails, the next in a French braid. Am I a kid or am I a hotshot?"

My father wandered into the kitchen looking bemused. He said hello and wandered out as he had come.

"Did you ask your mother about whether your father was romantic or not?" Al asked me.

"I forgot," I said. "I will."

"I brought my sweats just in case we land another freebie," Al said. "I bet he gives us one."

"Bet you he won't."

"Five bucks," Al said. We shook on it. She owes me about a hundred bucks, but she says I owe her about two hundred, on bets alone. We never pay, we just bet.

When we finally started out, the sun had gone under a bunch of dark clouds and a cold wind had sprung up.

"Do you think this is real life?" Al asked me as we hurried to beat the rain. "This, I mean," and she made a lavish gesture that took in our surroundings: the street, the buildings, the city. "Is this the real world or is it a fake?"

It's a good thing I was used to her mood swings, otherwise I couldn't handle them.

"It's as real as you make it, I guess," I said.

"Suppose it's not real, suppose it's phony," Al said. Her mood had darkened, along with the sky. "Suppose we never find out what the real world is like. Suppose we keep on fooling ourselves that we're kids, but we grow up, get out of school, make lots of money in jobs we love, get married, have kids, and that's it."

"Whaddaya mean, that's it?" I said. "That sounds like quite a lot."

"Maybe I want more out of life," she said.

"That's why we're going to Al's Health Club," I said. "So you can have more. More abs, more pecs, more gluts, and a much, much tighter behind," and I sped along the pavement as fast as I could so she couldn't catch up with me.

"Help ya?" asked a burly lady behind the desk, wearing a peaked hat with NAPA written across the front and a set of earphones attached.

"Is Al here?" we asked her.

"Al?" For a second her roving glance lit on us and she even smiled. Then she looked over our heads as if she was searching for Al in the corners. "I think he's in back. Things are kinda rocky, what with deliveries and all. Stuff doesn't show up, he goes ape. Better not bother him today. He's like a gorilla today, a gorilla what just sat on an ant heap." The lady gave out a short, sharp laugh that sounded like a dog barking.

"How's business?" Al said.

"Good," the lady said, nodding vigorously. "Not bad, good. You shoulda been here yesterday. The joint was jumping. Saturdays are best. You get your money people in on Saturdays. They want to shape up, look sleek for a big night on the town. You get your bank presidents, your Madison Ave. types.

"Sundays, like today," the lady continued, "you get your basic weirdos. You wouldn't believe the weirdos Sundays bring in. Our clientele goes to church, we got a big church-going crowd, believe it or not. Sundays," the burly lady leaned over the counter, tapping one long, perfect, red nail against the glass, "are for weirdos. This morning I have a gentleman, he comes in and wants the machine he's using to face north so he faces north too when he's working out, so he can be aligned with the planets. That what he says, 'aligned with the planets.' You ever heard that before? No, me neither," she said, as if Al and I had spoken.

"They tell you all the nuts are in California these days," the burly lady went on, obviously wound up, "but don't you believe them. There are plenty of nuts in these parts, a lot of 'em around. They eat Sunday dinner, come down here to work it off. There's all these starving people we got, living in doorways and boxes

130

and all. They could use some of the dough these people spend on getting their bodies in shape. Think of the little kids who don't eat their supper on acount of there's no supper to eat. Think of it if you want to drive yourself nuts. Yes, darling. Help ya?" the burly lady said, calming down.

A lady in red stood in front of the desk, biting her lips.

"My fiancé lives in Seattle," she said, "and he only gets east once a month and I wondered if we could both use the same membership."

"Listen, darling," the burly lady said, "if it was up to me, you could bring your boyfriend any old time. But I'm not the boss lady. Check with Al. He's the boss. And like I'm telling these girls here, Al's a regular gorilla which sat on an ant heap today. Try him next week, why dontcha."

Al and I moved off and sat on a bench and watched people work out on the Nautilus machine.

"How about if I slip into the dressing room and into my sweats?" Al said.

"Try it. If it doesn't work, so you tried," I said.

We looked for Ms. Bolton, but she wasn't around. She'd said she might come on Sunday.

"Probably she's out on a blind date," Al said.

We'd decided to split and were halfway to the door when we saw Big Al come storming out of the back, his arms waving, eyes wild.

"Everybody outa here!" he shouted. He rushed toward us, swerving, flapping his arms like some kind of wounded bird.

"Out! Ya hear me? I said Out and I mean Out! All youse! Out!" As we watched, astounded and astonished, Al seemed to swell, as if he'd been filled with air. His face was practically purple.

Some people moved toward the door sideways, like crabs, keeping an eye on Al to make sure he kept his distance. Some stayed where they were, riding bicycles, running in place, working out with their eyes closed, paying him no mind. Lots of New Yorkers are used to bizarre behavior and don't let it get to them.

Still, several women scuttled into the dressing room and came out with their clothes clutched under their arms, not wanting to stop to change.

The burly lady with the headphones on her hat moved toward Al, not in any hurry. We saw her say something to him, then we saw him push her toward the door with a series of short, sharp jabs.

"Let's get out of here," I said.

"He's loco," Al said. "Either that or he's drunk."

"I don't think he's drunk," I said. "He sure looks funny, though."

"Maybe he's having a heart attack," Al said. All the time we were talking we were moving toward the door.

It seemed to me Al's face was turning purpler by the minute. I tried to think what that was a symptom of and couldn't. I didn't think it was anything the

Heimlich maneuver could help. I practice the Heimlich maneuver on Teddy quite a lot, when he lets me, because if ever I'm in a restaurant and somebody chokes on a piece of steak, I plan to save his life. Or hers, of course.

The rush of cold air felt good on our faces. We stood on the sidewalk, undecided, looking back at the health club. Several angry stragglers joined us, talking to anyone who would listen.

"We pay good money, you think he'd treat us right, right?" a man said. "What's with the guy? He's loony, if you ask me. They oughta come and haul him to Bellevue. I wouldn't come back here if he got on his knees and begged me. There are plenty of fitness places you can go, have a relaxing workout, tone yourself up. Who needs it."

"Maybe we should stick around," I said.

"Nah." Al started walking toward Third Avenue. "No sense hanging around. I bet all it is is he had a fight with his wife and she called him up and said 'Get your buns home, else I toss the pot roast out the window.' "

"You think?" I wasn't convinced.

"Sure. It's something simple like that," Al said. "Marital discord is rife. You're lucky your mother and father don't fight."

"They do," I said. "Only they fight quietly."

"That's the neatest trick of the week," Al told me.

A long, shiny limo cruised down the street toward us, as black and sleek as a snake.

"Whaddya want to bet that's some celeb who heard about Al's freebie and he's going there now to check it out," Al said. "Boy, is he in for a shock."

Al and I turned to watch as the limo slowed in front of the health club. Maybe Al was right, maybe it was Elizabeth Taylor or Woody, up for a free workout. Woody sure could use one. So could Liz, if you ask me.

The window on the passenger side rolled down slowly and an arm came out. There was something in the arm's hand. With one quick, expert toss, the something sailed out the window of the car and shattered the window of Al's Health Club with a tremendous roar. Flames shot up and the building shook.

"Down!" Al shouted and pulled me into the shelter of a nearby doorway.

We hit the deck, the way they do on TV. My nose scraped the pavement and began to bleed.

The street was filled with noise. People ran back and forth, mouths wide, eyes wild. Some ran as fast as their feet would carry them, crouching low, making themselves small.

"What is it! It's a bomb! It's the Russians!" Those were some of the things we heard.

"Look! Up there!" One man paused in his flight and pointed to the sky. "It's one of them bombers, long-range bombers. See?" and he shook the little boy in his arms. "See, up there. Sooner or later, it had to happen."

Al and I cowered in the doorway. Blood dripped out of my nose. Someone tapped on the glass. We looked up. A face was pushed against the pane, distorting the features.

"Get outa here!" the face hollered. "I want no trouble here. Get outa here or I'll call the cops!"

Al and I clutched one another.

I put a hand on my nose.

"I think it was a fire bomb," Al whispered. The face was still there and words came out of its mouth, but we huddled there, not knowing what to do, where to go.

We heard a key rattling in the lock. The person was coming to get us. Al took my hand and pulled me out of the doorway and down the block.

"Someone threw a fire bomb at Al's Heath Club and it just missed us," Al said, struggling to stay cool.

"My mother said be home before dark," I said. "We better get home right away. It's almost dark."

Al gave me a strange look.

"The sun just came out," she said.

I felt very cold.

"I don't care what you say," I told her. "I'm going home. My mother worries about me if I'm not home in time. I don't want her to worry about me."

We heard the sirens. It sounded as if every ambulance and fire engine and police car in the entire city was racing to where we were.

"I'm going," I said, but I didn't move. My feet were made of lead.

Al put her hand to her head. "My hair's burning," she said. "I can smell it."

The whole block smelled of fire.

"Come on," I said, tugging at her sleeve.

To my surprise, she came along.

We wobbled homeward. Halfway there, Al stopped dead.

"I wonder if Al's O.K.," she said.

"They'll take care of him," I said.

"Pretend nothing happened, when we get home," Al said.

"She didn't want to let me go," I said. "My mother didn't want to let me go."

Al didn't seem to hear me. Her eyes were huge as she poked a thumb behind us and said, "You want real life, that's real."

"You were the one who wanted real," I reminded her. I felt as if I might be sick. "Now that you know what real's like, maybe you better settle for make-believe."

Eighteen

"Pretend nothing happened," Al whispered. As the door opened, I could hear my mother and father talking in the kitchen.

"Just pretend nothing happened," Al said again, very tense, very anxious. She kept running her fingers through her bangs, checking to see if they were stilll there. She was driving me crazy, doing that. Stop, I wanted to say. Stop. Stop. I didn't have the strength.

Be cool, I told myself. I moved my shoulders to loosen them up. Get cool and stay there. Impossible.

"Hi," I said, standing in the hall, not wanting to go all the way into the brightly lit room.

"Here we are," Al said.

"What on earth happened to you?" my mother asked. She put down the spoon she was holding. My father was taking something out of the oven.

"You're just in time," he said.

"I'll make some tea," my mother said. She always makes tea in a crisis.

"No, thanks," I said.

Before I swallowed anything, I'd have to get rid of the lump in my throat.

"Could I please have a glass of water?" Al said.

My mother got it for her.

"Sit down," she said. We sat at the kitchen counter.

"I'd like some ice cream, please," I said. "How about you, Al? Want some?"

Al nodded. Her bangs looked strange. Usually they lie flat on her forehead. Now they stuck straight out, as if she had on her homemade head band, which she didn't.

"Is your mother home, Al?" my father said.

"No," she said. "I don't think so. She told me where she was going, but I don't remember what she said. Maybe she's at a matinee with Stan."

"What's your number?" My father went to the telephone. Al told him and he dialed and let the phone ring quite a long time before hanging up.

"Maybe she's taking a tub," I said.

Teddy wandered in, looked at us, and blinked.

"You guys get caught in a tornado?" he said.

Trust Teddy.

"Shut up," I said.

Teddy slitted his little eyes at us.

"You look like you got totaled in an avalanche," he said.

"Mom, can't you make him shut up?" I said. "He makes my head hurt, he talks so much."

"Teddy, I think it might be a good idea if you turned the TV on," my father said. Teddy gawked. This was a first, all right. Usually he was told it would be a good idea if he turned the TV off.

"What happened to her nose?" I heard Teddy say as my father propelled him out of the kitchen. "She get caught in a dog fight or something?"

My mother gave us tea and ice cream, without an argument. It was mint chocolate chip. I put a spoonful of ice cream into my tea and watched it disintegrate. It didn't taste too bad. I'd never tried putting ice cream into hot tea before.

My spoon made a loud noise in my cup. Al drank her water, then ate some ice cream. I could hear her swallowing.

"You're home early," my mother said after a long silence. She kept swabbing down the counters with a sponge, although they looked perfectly clean to me.

"You want to talk about it?" she asked. "Tell us what happened."

"No," I said.

"Actually," Al said, "it was kind of bizarre. Not your basic Sunday-afternoon outing, if you get me. There was this enormous limo coming down the street, and somebody threw something out the window and there was this gigantic burst of flame and a big loud noise. Like a bomb going off."

She got off the stool and began to pace.

"Of course, I've never heard a real live bomb go off before," she said. "I've only experienced it in the movies or on the tube. But it was definitely a bomb, probably a fire bomb. I've read about fire bombs. He went around shouting for everybody to get out, flapping his arms and acting sort of crazy."

Al pushed her bangs back so they stuck up straight. She looked funny, but I didn't laugh.

"He knew, I guess," Al said. "Somebody warned him. Otherwise, it might've got us."

My mother went after an imaginary spot on the counter as if it had been a rodent. Or a cockroach.

"The good Lord was watching out for you," she said.

"Good Lord, heck," I said. "It was Al watching out for us. That's his name, Al. He owns the health club. He gave us a freebie. We took our teacher, Ms. Bolton, too. We worked out and everything. He's looking for word-of-mouth customers. He just opened."

Al licked her hand and ran it over her bangs.

"You can't kid me," she said. "It was the mob. Bet you anything. Bet you a thousand big ones," she said to me.

"Sure," I said.

"That's just the kind of thing the mob's famous for,"

Al went on. "It's on TV all the time. You do something they don't like, they fire-bomb you. Those bozos don't fool around."

My father stood in the doorway, listening.

"Do you think I should call the doctor?" my mother asked my father.

He shook his head. "They're all right," he said. "They'll be fine."

I wanted to lie down in the worst way, but I knew if I did my mother would freak.

"Let's play Russian Bank," I said to Al.

"What?" she said.

"Russian Bank," I said. "Like we played last night."

"No, thanks," Al said. "I think I'll go home and take a shower. I feel sort of dirty."

"I'll go with you," my mother said. "I don't think you should be alone right now."

"I'm fine, really," Al said. "Thanks anyway, but I'm really fine."

I went to the door with her.

"I'm not telling my mother anything," she said fiercely. "She can't handle violence. Mum's the word." And she laid a finger on her lips.

Al was halfway down the hall when the elevator door opened. Out came Al's mother and a man. That must be Stan, I thought. He's not so cute.

"Well, hello!" Al's mother said gaily. She was smiling and laughing and having a good time with Stan.

Al tucked her head down and fumbled for her key.

"Hi, Ma," she mumbled.

"Alexandra," her mother cried. "What on earth's happened to you? Look at you. Something bad has happened. Tell me."

It was on the evening news.

The reporter was new; young and blond and sounding like Diane Sawyer. I think there's a school they go to where they all learn to sound like Diane Sawyer.

"A health club on New York's Upper East Side was fire-bombed this afternoon," she said. "No one was seriously injured, although several people were treated at the scene. The club's owner, Albert Anaconda, alias Big Al Carlucci, alias Allan Smith, managed to warn the patrons so they could get out before the bomb hit. He'd been warned in an anonymous telephone call that the place was going to be hit by a fire bomb. It is thought the bombing was perpetrated by members of the mob. Mr. Anaconda had mob connections and apparently was behind in his monthly payments on a debt. The bombing was a warning that if he didn't pay up, more bombing would follow. Mr. Anaconda was taken to the hospital for treatment, and the police are questioning him further. The health club had been in operation for only a short time. Damage was extensive. For further details, tune in at eleven tonight."

The blond reporter smiled. Maybe it was the real Diane Sawyer, I thought. Hard to tell.

Teddy's eyes never left my face.

"It was Mafia business," he said.

"Enough, Teddy," my father said.

"Mafia, mafia, mafia," Teddy muttered under his breath.

"I better call Craig," Teddy said when the news program was over. "He won't believe it. Craig'll flip. He thinks the Mafia's only up in Connecticut. Wait'll he hears you got bombed by the real Mafia right here in New York City. The real thing."

"If I call him," Teddy said, "will you tell him? If I tell him, he'll probably think I'm making it all up. If you tell him, he'll believe you. Will you, please?"

I lay back on the couch. My mother had put some stuff on my nose and it felt better. I was being treated like a princess. Teddy had said please. This was a day and a night for the books.

"It's Polly on the phone," my mother said. "Do you feel like talking?"

"Sure," I said.

"Hi, Pol," I said. "What's new?" Then I waited for her to say "Not much, what's new with you."

"Listen, turkey," she said instead, "are you or are you not going to this tea dance? You and Al have stalled long enough, and Harry says he's psyched up to take Thelma. What's more, Thelma's got a new dress and everything. You guys have to make up your minds."

"A lot's happened to me since I saw you last, Pol,"

I told her. I made my voice sound weary, very weary. "Don't give me heat. Al and I were fire-bombed this afternoon and her bangs got singed and my nose got beat up. I'm O.K., but Al's sorta shook up."

There was a silence, then Polly said, "You putting me on?"

"No, I'm not putting you on," I said. "It's what happened. It was on television. If you want further details, tune in at eleven."

"Where's Al?" Polly said after a pause.

"She's home. Taking a shower, I imagine."

"Was anybody killed or anything?" Polly said. "I mean, where'd this happen? Were you just walking down the street and somebody threw a fire bomb at you or what?"

"It was at this health club Al and I went to," I said. "We got out in the nick of time. It said on the news they think it was Mafia doings."

"If I find out you're putting me on," Polly said, "you're in trouble."

"Cross my heart and hope to die, Pol," I told her.

"It was a big weekend for Al and me," I went on. "First, we had blind dates last night at a party. From Cincinnati. I'm all burned out. It was wild."

"No kidding? What happened?" Polly asked.

"Not a heck of a lot," I said. "It was the dialogue. I'll tell you all about it when I see you. I'm not sure Al's up for another blind date, though. She's burned out too, plus her bangs are singed and they look funny.

It wasn't love at first sight. The blind date, I mean. My father says it almost never is."

"I'll stall Harry another day, then," Polly said, "Tell Al tomorrow's D day, though. Thelma's on stand-by, don't forget. Harry's plenty psyched. He's never known anyone named Thelma before. He thinks it's kind of cute."

"I bet he's never known a girl named Al before either," I said. "That oughta psyche him right out of his head."

"Good point," Polly said.

Nineteen

In the morning I called Al.

"You going to school today?" I said.

"Listen," she said. "I trimmed off the singed parts and I must've dropped about ten pounds yesterday. I look gorge. Sure I'm going."

We met at the elevator.

"My mother said maybe I should stay home today," I told her.

"Mine too," Al said. "I guess they think we're wimps, that we can't take the stress of daily life in the big city. Little do they know. We have to go and inform the troops of the battle in progress, *n'est-ce pas?*"

The elevator door creaked open, revealing Sparky and his mom. Sparky was sulking, probably because he was on his leash. He hates his leash. His mom says he doesn't like to be confined.

"Hello," we said. Sparky's mom waggled fingers at us in greeting.

If only the elevator had been crowded, we could've said we'd wait for the next one. But it was just us and her. And him.

We got on.

"Thank you for a nice time," Al said right off. "We looked around for you to say good-bye, but we couldn't see you. It was a nice party."

Her mother would've been proud of her.

I nodded and smiled agreement.

"Well," Sparky's mom said, "a party is what gets the blood stirring. What are one's friends for if not to come to one's parties? We must all hang together or we hang alone. Isn't that right? Josh loved meeting you girls. He said he just loved it. He had the best time. Isn't he a darling boy? His friend is too. What was his name? Oh, I'm so bad about names. Some days I can hardly remember my own. I'm off to the beauty salon. I feel the need of a facial. I must drop Sparky off at his day-care center. They love him there. They just think he's the cutest thing. He's such a dear little one, isn't he?"

Al and I both smiled. Behind Sparky's mom's back, Al rested the toe of her sneaker on Sparky's head. He lifted his lips and sneered, then he raised his eyebrow at her too. Sparky has only one eyebrow, which stretches across both little eyes. It's one of the things that makes him so outstanding.

"We'll do it again soon, girls," Sparky's mom said.

"Not on your tintype," I said, under my breath.

"Just think." We stopped at Lexington for the light. "We're lucky to be alive." Al was very serious. "We might be dead. We owe Big Al a big debt."

"Maybe we should send him some flowers," I said.

"That's a good idea," Al said. "I wonder what name we should use? I mean, he's got all those aliases. Maybe instead of sending flowers, we should visit him in the hospital."

"What hospital is he in?" I said.

Al shrugged. "We can stop by the health club today after school and ask. They'll probably know."

"You think the health club is still there?" I said. "I mean, a fire bomb usually levels everything it hits, doesn't it?"

"I don't know," Al said. She so seldom says "I don't know" I was momentarily flabbergasted.

"Polly called last night," I said. "She says Thelma's on standby for the tea dance. She has a new dress and everything, and Polly says her cousin Harry is all psyched up about Thelma because he's never known a girl with that name before and he thinks it's kind of cute."

"Harry sound like a twerp," Al said.

"Well, Polly says we've stalled long enough," I told Al. "She says we have to decide today if we're going. Do you want to go to the tea dance on a blind date or don't you?"

"No," Al said. "If I knew how to tea-dance, I might. But I haven't the faintest idea, so I'm not going. Furthermore, my experience with blind dates has probably warped me for time immemorial."

Trouble was, I wanted to go. But I wasn't going without Al.

"As a matter of fact," Al went on, "my experience with blind dates has not only warped me, it has probably ruined my life. I may never get married, have two kids and a station wagon and a Jacuzzi in my bathroom. Or a sauna in the backyard, in addition to a Weber cooker for barbecues. Do you realize what one terrible blind date can do? It can louse you up forevermore."

"I didn't think it was *that* bad," I said.

"My standards are much higher than yours," Al told me. "I want a blind date to have manners. I want him to stand up, not loll all over on account of if he stands up he'll blow his midget cover.

"Besides," Al said, "I don't have anything to wear to a tea dance."

"The dress you wore to your birthday party would be terrific," I said. "That dress is very becoming."

"You sound just like my mother," Al said. "If I wore that taffeta dress, then you'd wear your taffeta dress and we'd look like a mother-daughter combo. I'm the mother and you're the daughter. I look much older than you. That's because I'm stout. Stout people tend to look older than skinny ones."

"I'm not skinny," I protested.

"Where does that leave me, then?" Al said.

"What happened to you?" Martha Moseley screeched. "You get caught in a bear trap?"

Martha's vassals, lined up single file behind her, tittered.

"The bomb got my nose is all," I said. "Watch TV for further developments." Before I knew Al, I never would've been able to handle Martha Moseley.

"Ms. Bolton," Al said, "did you know Al's Health Club was fire-bombed yesterday? It just missed us."

Ms. Bolton's eyes got wide. "I was planning to go there to work out yesterday," she said. "Then my fiancé turned up and we went to the zoo instead."

"Your fiancé!" Al said.

"We didn't know you were engaged," I said. "We were planning on fixing you up with a nice blind date, only we couldn't find one."

"I'm getting married at Christmas," Ms. Bolton said. "Here." She took a snapshot out of her wallet and showed it to us.

"He's a hunk," Al said.

"He's very good looking," I told Ms. Bolton.

"Thanks," she said.

We went by the health club on our way home. It

was boarded up and there were police standing around, in case of looters, they told us. They didn't know anything or, if they did, they weren't telling us.

"I have to call Polly and tell her if we're going or not," I said.

"If you want to go, go," Al said. "But count me out."

"I'm going," I said. "I'm calling Polly and telling her I'm going."

"So go," Al said. "Go ahead."

I knew she didn't really think I'd go without her. It was time I taught her a lesson.

"Me and Thelma will make quite a pair," I said. "She's incredibly shallow, but shallow in a deep way, if you get my meaning."

"You'll be sorry," Al said. "All right for you, go."

"Don't be a sorehead, sorehead," I said.

Twenty

I'd just dished up the instant pudding when Al's special ring came.

Two, then one, then two.

"It's Al!" Teddy shouted. "I'll get it!"

Usually we fight to be the one who'll let Al in. This time I let Teddy go. He was halfway to the door before he realized he had a clear field.

"What's up?" Teddy said. "It's Al."

"So what?" I said. "Big deal."

"Hey, Al." Teddy opened the door a crack and peered out, making sure it really *was* Al. "It's you, isn't it?"

"Sure thing, Ted," Al said. Then she looked at me

and said, "Two things. I heard on the news that Al's Health Club is closed due to bankruptcy and damages due to the fire. He's suffering from first- and second-degree burns, but he's in satisfactory condition. The police are waiting to question him."

She stopped and stood there with her hands behind her back.

"What's the second thing?" I said.

"This." She brought a magazine out that she'd been hiding. "You call Polly yet?"

"I was just about to," I lied. Actually, I'd taken the phone off the hook right after my mother and father went out to the movies. I didn't want to talk to Polly until I knew what I was going to say.

"O.K." Al cleared her throat. "I came across something in this magazine I want to read to you."

"Shoot," I said.

"Here goes." Al cleared her throat again.

"We're talking here about the Weimar era in Germany," she said. "Circa 1919 to 1933. This was the period between the two World Wars, before Hitler really got going. I'm quoting an old German actress who was a young German actress at that time and remembers it well. She says 'There was a great deal of freedom at that time, to do anything people wanted. Intellectual freedom as well as personal freedom, sexual freedom. There were many things going on at that time that might be considered outrageous in this day and age. For instance, nude tea dances were not uncommon, taking place at many of the big hotels in Berlin.' "

She looked at me.

"What?" I said.

"That's what it said. 'Nude tea dances.' "

She waited. I kept my face blank.

"So?" I said.

"Don't give me that 'so' routine," Al said. "First, you get the mental picture." She began to pace.

"They've got their little white gloves on, see. They've also got their little hats with their little veils on, and the men are wearing garters to hold up their socks. Get it? Is it lovely? It's so wonderful I can't stand it." Al hugged the magazine to her chest.

"They go to this snazzy hotel, sort of like the Plaza," she said, darting a look at me, then at Teddy, who was polishing off the pudding and couldn't care less.

"How do they get to the hotel?" I said. It was kind of fascinating to contemplate the logistics of it all. "In a car, or maybe their chauffeur drives them and lets them out at the front door. They've got their fur-lined overcoats on, probably, because it's cold. It's winter, see. Do they take off their duds when they get to the hotel, or are they already nude under their fur-lined coats?"

Al was silent, looking at me to see where this was taking me.

"No," I said, frowning thoughtfully. "I think they go to the mens' and ladies' rooms and take off their clothes and put 'em in a brown paper bag and leave 'em with the check girl. Where they also check their hats and coats."

"I think they're nude when they arrive at the hotel," Al told me. "Then when they take off their hats and coats and check 'em with the girl, there they are, standing there, starkers."

We were quiet, thinking about it.

"I wonder if they've got shoes on?" I said. "Sure. Because if they didn't wear shoes and somebody stepped on their feet, their toes would get crushed. Shoes are a must."

Al began to dance around the room.

"How about the music?" she said.

"Probably rock or country," I said.

Al stopped dancing.

"Hey, baby, we're talking 1919 to 1933 here," she reminded me. "Long before rock and country days. And it's Germany. They played waltzes, most likely. You get the picture? There they are, starkers, with their gloves and hats and shoes on, and they're waltzing, waltzing around the dance floor. Talking and chatting and laughing. Having a grand time. Starkers every step of the way. I mean, I could die. It's so absolutely wonderful I can't stand it.

"It is so gorgeous!" Al chortled. "So perfect. Even in my wildest dreams, I couldn't have made it up."

"When they whip off their coats and hats and hand 'em to the hat-check girl," I said, "is she nude too?

Or has she got on a neat little black dress with a white collar and all?"

"Who knows?" Al said.

Teddy looked up from his dish of pudding. He scraped his spoon noisily around, getting up the last good bits.

"I bet they played fast music," he said. "That must've been pretty funny, when they played fast music."

Al and I looked at each other.

"Let's call Polly," Al said. "Tell her we're going."

Twenty-One

It was late, almost ten. Teddy was pounding his ear and I was just getting into bed, when I heard Al's ring.

"Pete's sake," I said. "What's she want now?"

I opened the door.

Al stood there.

"Your mother and father home yet?" she whispered.

"No, but they will be," I said. "Any minute."

"I just wanted to show you what I'm wearing to the tea dance," Al said. She had on her Mother Zandi turban and she'd drawn circles of rouge on her cheeks to make herself look glamorous. Her eyebrows were thick and black and made her look like Groucho Marx.

She had on some sort of long, billowy shirt. Her arms were crossed on her chest.

"Are you ready?" Al said.

"Hurry up," I said.

She flung her arms wide. The big shirt parted. Underneath, Al was all flesh. Nude.

"You're cuckoo," I gasped, trying not to laugh.

"How do you like it?" Al said.

I reached out and touched her.

"It's my mother's flesh-colored bodysuit. Pretty classy, huh?"

"You are totally out to lunch," I told her.

We heard the elevator coming up.

"I've gotta split," Al said.

She zipped down the hall.

"Have a weird day," I called softly.

The elevator stopped at our floor.

"I already did," she said. "Adios." And she was gone.

Twenty-Two

"Nada," Al said over her shoulder. She was hanging out our dining room window, checking to see if our dates were approaching.

"Except for a skinny little bowlegged person down there, looks like he might be yours," Al said.

My mother would have a cow.

"Get back in here, " I said. I was nervous. We were fourteen floors up. If Al fell out, her mother would most likely sue.

The telephone rang. I got there first. It was Polly. With a bulletin.

"They're on their way," Polly said. "They're not coming empty-handed, either. They're bringing corsages for you and Al."

"Oh gross!" I said. "Corsages!"

Al bounced in from the window.

"Corsages?" she said in a hollow voice. "Grand-mothers love corsages. They pin 'em on their chests when they go out to dinner on Mother's Day. I'm not wearing any corsage. If I have to wear a corsage to a thé dansant, I'm not going."

"Al says she's not going if she has to wear a cor-sage," I told Polly.

"What kind of corsage?" Al said, grabbing the phone from me.

Polly told her.

"Well, at least they're not orchids,"Al said. "I draw the line at orchids."

"Hang up," I told her. "In case they're trying to call to tell us your date fell under a truck and broke his leg and his friend has to help him to the hospital."

"You think that's a possibility?" Al said, her face brightening.

The doorbell rang.

Al froze. I skinned into the bathroom and locked the door.

Al pounded on the bathroom door. "It's only your mother," she said. "She forgot her key."

"Is that all?" I said, emerging calm, cool, and col-lected.

"I'm going to be sick," Al said.

"No you're not," I told her."It's all in your mind."

"I better go to the bathroom," Al said.

My mother stood there, looking at us. "God forbid

they don't have bathrooms at this tea dance," she said.

"Do you think this is a rite of passage?" Al asked her.

"I'm afraid so," my mother said.

The doorbell rang again.

"Ooooh." Al held her head.

"Pull yourselves together and I'll go and let them in." My mother smoothed her hair and arranged her sweetsy smile. "I'll tell them you're not quite ready. Then I'll come to tell you they've arrived and give you a quick but comprehensive rundown."

"Mine's the midget," Al told her. "Don't spare my feelings. Just level with me right off the bat, O.K.?"

My mother went out. We heard her introduce herself, heard them introduce themselves. We both went and sat down on my bed.

My mother glided in, looking pleased with herself.

"How tall is the midget?" Al said.

"They're both cute as bugs," my mother said. "Oh, and I'd say they're both tall. About so high," and she lifted her hand six inches from the top of her own head. "Perfectly darling, both of them. You ready?"

"No," we said in unison.

"Listen. Get out there. They're pretty cute. Lovely manners too. Pull up your socks and get going. Trust me."

I opened the door and put one foot out. I could feel Al's hand in the middle of my back, pushing me.

"Here goes," I said.